BELLA FAYRE

GUARDIAN OF THE DAMNED

A Donna DeShayne Adventure

Beckey!
Blessings...
Bella Fayre
'19

Praise for *Guardian of the Damned*

"*Guardian of the Damned* proves Bella Fayre knows how to weave a spine-tingling tale. Donna DeShayne has to sidestep attempts on her life while searching for a serial killer. In the end all questions are answered in one surprising twist after another."

—Rebecca Bridges, author, *After the Reunion*

"Bella Fayre is among the stellar authors writing mystery today who has the ability to keep you riveted chapter after chapter. Her talent is enormous and never predictable."

—Ann Jeffries, author, *Walking On Uneven Ground*

"Guardian of the Damned is engaging and hard to put down. Fayre's easy style and solid characters make this mystery yet another success in her series."

—Carole O'Neil, author, *Hidden Truth*

"A cleverly written suspense story that will have you racing to the end."

—Amy Quonce, author, *A Family No More*

"Bella Fayre is becoming my new favorite author! *Guardian of the Damned,* her latest, is too good to put down even for a moment! Once I read the first page, I couldn't stop until I finished the book."

—J.A. Meinecke, author, *A Woman to Reckon With*

"Bella Fayre has another winner with *Guardian of the Damned*. The author captivates and holds the reader with engaging characters and a storyline full of twists and turns."

—Nancy Engle, author, *Murder at Mount Joy* and *Image of Perfection*

Bellafayre@ucanpublishing.com

Printed and Bound in the United States of America

Published and Distributed By
UCAN Publishing, LLC
P.O. Box 51616
Myrtle Beach, S.C. 29579
www.ucanpublishing.com

Proofreading:
EV Proofreading
www.evproofreading.com

Editing, Interior Layout, and Cover Design by:
Jessica Tilles/TWA Solutions
www.twasolutions.com

Converted ISBN: 978-0-9909310-3-4

Library of Congress Control Number: 2016941483

First Print: October 2016

Dedicated to the enduring spirit of

Johnstown, Pennsylvania

"...But if you are doing wrong, then you will have cause to fear them; it is not for nothing that they hold the power of the sword, for they are God's agents of punishment bringing retribution on the offender."

—Romans 13:4, *The Revised English Bible*

Chapter One

It had been meticulously planned for months and now finally executed. Another flawless culmination of diligent homework and fact-finding. Nonetheless, an additional check was performed just to be sure. It was foolish to grow too confident, even dangerous. When satisfied every detail had been accounted for, things were gathered.

Once home, a shower and change of clothes was paramount. Clothing would fall in the tub after stripping. One couldn't be too careful. Clothing and even boots would be placed in a plastic bag, and later burned. Never assume!

After showering, a visit to the cupboard was in order. Retrieved was a fifty-year-old bottle of Scotch. One drink in celebration was all that was needed. After all, it was only once a year! Pouring a drink and taking a slow, easy swallow, the eyes closed until the golden liquid found its way down the throat and to the stomach, producing glowing warmth that spread throughout. Supremely satisfied, the bottle was returned to the cupboard, with a silent promise to return to it again next year.

The cautious side proved to be an advantage. It had served well these past twenty-one years. No one suspected. No one had guessed. They were all fools! Enough clues had been given, not once, but twenty-one times!

The sense of accomplishment grew with each successful event. The task was not undertaken lightly. The mere possibility had been ignored for many years. The need for retribution, however, became too strong. After all, the losses had been devastatingly great. The unspoken cry for justice had been building. Finally heard, the anguish of many would be addressed, once and for all! There was no other way!

Chapter Two

Six Months Later

They reached for each other in the wee hours of the morning just before the faint light of dawn. As if it were the first time, their entwined bodies writhed in lustful ecstasy and mutual satisfaction before the primal moans of passion peaked in a shared release signaling a glorious oneness. After ten years, their bed-zest showed no signs of slowing down.

After a final snuggle and sultry kiss, Donna DeShayne rolled over to go back to sleep. This was Sunday. She always slept late on Sunday. Ken Daniels, after a time, released his tender embrace of her and quietly slipped out of bed to put on the coffee.

Ken was forever mesmerized by the hold she still had on him, and no less so this morning. What a lucky man he was, he mused. They found each other! That's all he knew. By providence or by luck, they'd found each other. They had often shared how their love was an exquisite rendering of two souls seeking each other for untold life times. These past ten years bore memories drenched in blessings of love, family, friends, and careers. While they had decided not to marry, their union was complete, unshakeable, and undying. It was what dreams were made of. Her past was another matter, but all was quiet and uneventful in that respect, and had been for all these years. Still, he remained watchful.

"Aunt Donna? Where are you?" the lilting voice of ten-year-old Mary Larson came from the back door.

"In the kitchen, honey!" Donna turned from the counter, ready to embrace her redheaded niece.

"We're here!" Mary gleefully shouted as she ran into the warm and welcoming embrace of her Aunt Donna.

"I am so excited you are spending the day with us!" Donna said while wrapping her niece in her arms and twirling her around several times.

"Are you giving out more than one of those? The hug, I mean, not the spinning." Mary's grandmother, Carole Tandermann asked, as she entered the kitchen, carrying bags and a tray.

"I have as many hugs as you need," Donna replied, embracing her best friend in welcome after helping set down her things.

"The little princess and her dutiful slave have arrived bearing food for today's barbecue. We did the deviled eggs this morning. I figured we would work on the salads here."

"Grandpa's coming later with the desserts!" Mary shared excitedly while looking outside the kitchen window for her Uncle Ken.

Ken was doing yard work when Mary and Carole arrived. He had promised Mary on her last visit she could ride on the lawn tractor with him. He was not about to renege, nor would the little redhead allow him to forget his promise, that he knew for sure. Mary was a bright, cheerful, if not insistent and determined little girl. Everyone loved her!

Mary heard Ken enter through the back door, and ran to him with outstretched arms and a smile a mile wide.

"How is our little girl?" Ken asked, picking her up in a warm embrace while smothering her with kisses.

"Uncle Ken! Did you forget? I'm not a little girl anymore!"

"No, you are not! Thank you for reminding me. It's just so hard to watch you grow up so fast," Ken replied, as he carried Mary into the kitchen, putting her down as he entered, but not before giving her another kiss, and one to her grandmother as well.

"Do you remember your promise?" she asked precociously while twirling a curl in her red hair. It was the look no adult could resist and she knew it.

"Now, Mary. Let Uncle Ken catch his breath," Carole gently admonished her granddaughter.

Ken approached Donna, kissing her good morning, before pouring a cup of coffee for himself.

"What promise would that be?" Ken teased with his back to Mary still holding his sight on Donna. It was all Carole and Donna could do to hide their grins.

"Uncle Ken! You know! I'm to help you mow the grass on the riding lawn mower today!"

"Oh, *that* promise. I have her all gassed up and ready to go. I think you need to change your clothes, though, my big girl. It's not usual to mow the grass in a dress, especially such a pretty one."

"She insisted on wearing her new dress this morning. I have play clothes she can change into," Carole explained, handing a light bag to the little girl. "Mary, why don't you change into your short set while Uncle Ken drinks his coffee? He'll wait for you."

Mary looked at her uncle for confirmation. When he nodded, she took off in a run toward the bathroom to change clothes.

"She gets prettier every time I see her," Donna said when Mary left the kitchen.

"And more talkative! I swear she can talk forever. Gavin and I are exhausted by the questions that never end. Yet, we wouldn't change a thing! What a blessing she has been!"

Carole and Gavin Tandermann were not really Mary's grandparents. They had assumed the role when Mary was just a baby, and they never regretted their decision, finding immeasurable pleasure in assisting with her care. Carole and Gavin had never had children, so being adopted as grandparents was especially thrilling.

Donna and Ken took on the role of aunt and uncle when Mary's mother, formerly Lacy Sue Sellers, became Donna's emotionally challenged patient ten years ago. Dr. Donna DeShayne, a forensic psychiatrist, met Lacy Sue in the course of a local murder investigation when asked by Detective Ken Daniels to assist. The victim turned out to be Lacy Sue's abusive husband, Joshua Aaron Sellers. Lacy Sue was hospitalized for serious injuries discovered at the scene of the horrific crime. The more puzzling concern, however, was that of her mind. She remained catatonic until a breakthrough was achieved. From that point on,

Donna worked with Lacy Sue diligently, patiently leading her to a state of mental stabilization and wholeness.

Before too long, Lacy Sue married her former high school friend, Saul Larson. In the course of Lacy Sue's treatment, Donna had many occasions to be with little Mary and Saul. He was devoted to his wife and daughter. In time, with the encouragement of her husband, Donna, Ken, and the Tandermanns, Lacy Sue earned a degree in nursing. She accepted a position at a local assisted living facility. Saul began a landscaping business, which was currently flourishing.

It was Carole and Gavin, however, who provided the Larsons a home until they were able to get one of their own, and the moral support the young couple needed at the time. The Larson family was devoted to Carole and Gavin, and they to them. Their ties were stronger than most families.

"How's Gavin this morning?" Donna asked her best friend.

"He's in his element! Baking cookies and creating exotic desserts for this afternoon. I was banned from the kitchen, which suits me fine. As long as I'm not banned from the bedroom!"

Donna let out a giggle. Carole was forever bragging about their bedroom gymnastics. Gavin was fifteen years older than Carole and had suffered a major heart attack five years earlier. Carole later confessed Gavin had his heart attack while they were making love. It turned out, such events were not altogether uncommon, but it was a detail Donna could have done without.

It was Gavin's heart attack that showed off Lacy Sue's potential for nursing. She never left his side while he was in the hospital, and visited every day while he recuperated at home, always bringing homemade soup or a heart-healthy dish. Carole was grateful for the support from her young friend. Gavin's heart attack had rocked Carole to her core. The thought of losing Gavin was paralyzing. Lacy Sue's consistent support, especially in the early weeks, provided Carole a respite.

"Is Lacy Sue in the kitchen as well?" Ken already knew the answer before he asked.

"She sure is! She and Saul arrived early this morning, bringing more clothes for Mary and baking supplies. You know Gavin and Lacy Sue—they are joined at the hip. She is the only one allowed in the kitchen while Gavin is creating. He even provides space for her at the counter. I call it 'The Flour Power Hour'!"

Donna and Ken roared. They could always count on Carole for her off-the-cuff humor. They were mindful it was Carole's devotion to Gavin, especially after his heart attack that led to her decision to give up her own psychiatric practice, turning most of her clients over to Donna. Carole's goal was to be more available to Gavin so they could travel. Carole also knew she needed to stay busy herself with something she loved to do, and so she had decided to open up a coffee shop, which she named simply *Beans*. Carole was a connoisseur of fine coffee. Any coffee! It was a rare sight for her to be without a mug of the dark nectar in her hand. The uniqueness of her shop brought people from all over as it offered coffee beans from around the world, freshly ground and brewed on the premises. One could take a pound, or two, home, or sit at one of the tables, order a cup of coffee of their choice, and choose from a selection of freshly baked goods. The shop was an instant success, open just six hours a day, from six in the morning to noontime. It was an easy operation to run, having the assistance of a very capable helper or two. Online sales propelled the business to another level of success with orders filled and shipped in the afternoons. The uniqueness of her operation saw Carole opening three more cafés in the community, with more planned. Donna and Ken often bragged of their friend's accomplishment.

Just then, Ken's cell phone rang. "Hey, buddy!" he greeted, obviously recognizing the voice on the other end. Donna watched the expression on his face, which was all smiles. "Hey, that's great! Glad you can make it. We'll see you both later. Let Karly's folks know they are welcome to join us. We'd love to see them again." When he ended the call he announced, "That was Jim Callahan. He and Karly got in last night. They're spending the long weekend with her parents. They'll be joining us for the barbecue."

Just then, Mary came bounding into the kitchen, looking cute in her jean shorts, red and white plaid shirt, and flaming red hair. "I'm ready, Uncle Ken! We need to get started! It's getting late and there's lots of work to be done."

"That there is, my little charmer!" Ken kissed Donna before taking Mary's hand and leading her out of the house to the riding lawn mower. Donna and Carole watched the two from the kitchen window for a couple of minutes. Ken and Mary were having a ball!

"I'm glad to know Jim and Karly are coming today. It's been a while since I've seen them. Ken has commented that he misses working with Jim," Donna shared.

"I guess the new job offer was too good to resist," Carole returned.

"Apparently. From what Ken says, Jim has settled in nicely and really enjoys the team he works with. I understand the pay and benefits are very good to boot."

Jim Callahan had served as a detective with Horry County, South Carolina Law Enforcement for the last five years, and twelve years before as a police officer in the county before moving to Pittsburgh, Pennsylvania, on the invitation of a high school friend of his to join the city's investigative branch. It was an exciting, but tough decision for Jim. He had finally given up his bachelor status when he met and fell in love with Karly West, a nurse practitioner. The couple married three years ago. The invitation to consider a move to Pittsburgh would mean they would be leaving family and friends, but they considered the move temporary, as they planned to come back to River Towne to retire when the time came. The increased pay and benefits, they reasoned, would go a long way in their retirement years. Karly was sure she could find another job in her field.

On the recommendation of Ken, Officer Caleb Blackwell, who had often assisted the detectives in investigative scenarios, filled the vacancy left by Jim. Caleb was as competent and professional as Jim, and proved to be a wise choice in filling the void. Caleb had married Sienna eight years earlier, and had two young sons, Paul and Samuel, who would often play with Mary Larson.

Their guests would be arriving mid-afternoon. The day was producing clear skies and somewhat milder weather after scorching temperatures a week earlier. Hosting a Fourth of July barbecue was a yearly event for Ken and Donna. The pool was cleaned, the grounds were mowed, tables and chairs had been set out, and Ken and Mary were busy placing mini American flags along the perimeter of the grounds in celebration. It would be good to be with friends again.

The highlight of the weekend would be the much-anticipated visit of Ken's daughter, Megan and son-in-law, Greg. Megan had married two years ago. Her husband, Greg Bishop, was a special education teacher she met when she accepted a position to teach at a local elementary school in River Towne. In time, Greg and Megan accepted teaching positions in New Jersey, where the demand for special needs teachers was great, and the pay was far beyond what they could realize in the county.

Ken's adjustment to Megan's move proved to be a challenge. He and his daughter were very close. While he understood she had a new husband and a new life, he struggled with her living so far away. Having her and Greg visit for the month of July elated both Ken and Donna. They would be arriving shortly. It was going to be a great party!

Chapter Three

The homework was done. It would be time soon. A check on the poisons would ensure success. There were several favorites at his disposal, and all easy to obtain if one knew how. The trick was successful administration and the use of one poison that would go undetected in a general screening.

The death of the first sixteen had been purposely chosen for their initial roles. The last five killings were meant to underscore arrogant disregard. How dare they cause such untold grief and get away with it!

How many more would be killed? There was simply no answer. Never planning to go beyond the original sixteen, the compulsion for revenge rose time and time again like a fever. It had to be quenched. So the killings continued.

Travel plans were made. All expenses would be paid in cash. No credit card trail. No one would question an absence. The killer frequently traveled and wouldn't be gone for more than two days. It was all part of the homework and careful planning guaranteeing success. Tonight a disguise would be decided. That was the fun part!

How enjoyable was the anonymity of a disguise! The collection was substantial; wigs, mustaches, beards, eyebrows, noses, fake scars, not to mention an array of clothing to complement the choice of persona.

Afterward the tracking of the discovery of the body and any ongoing investigation would be pursued by temporarily subscribing to the local online version of the newspaper in the town or city most likely to cover the event. How the killer loved the Internet! In the early years, there was the need to subscribe to the local newspaper several months ahead of the killing and stay subscribed for a time to find out details of any investigation if provided. A post office box was secured in a nearby town to receive newspapers for greater privacy. Having them home-delivered would raise questions. There was always the need to be careful. Supplies were sent to still another post office box. The occasions to receive supplies were infrequent, but ongoing vigilance proved essential.

Little time was spent at the kill site. It was calculated to almost the minute how much time after arrival to kill, check for loose ends, and leave undetected. It was why the killer had not been caught. Scrupulous attention to detail and timing was how so many murders had gone unsolved. One each year for twenty-one years!

Chapter Four

The barbecue was a huge success. Their guests, many of them friends from law enforcement and their families, had brought an array of dishes to complement the buffet table with endless choices of salads, cheeses, meats, relish trays, vegetable platters, and breads. The favorite selection by the group, however, was from Gavin's presentation of desserts, hands down!

The children played in the pool with adult supervision, while some of the adults played horseshoes or badminton. Others were content to sit around the pool or garden area conversing and enjoying each other's company.

Saul and Lacy Sue Larson took the occasion to announce they were expecting their second child. No one was more elated than Mary, who was told she was going to be a big sister. Gavin and Carole oozed with joy for the chance to grandparent another child. Perhaps the next child would have flaming red hair like Daddy and big sister.

The day of swimming and play left Mary exhausted. Carole and Gavin took her home with them for the night, letting Saul and Lacy Sue stay later to enjoy the party. It was way past her bedtime. Greg and Megan left shortly thereafter, but not before getting another hug from Ken.

The party thinned out by late evening, leaving Saul and Lacy Sue, along with Jim and Karly as the last to leave. Saul and Lacy Sue marveled at how fortunate they were to have found such supportive friends, and while Donna and Ken were not related to Saul and Lacy Sue in any way, their role as aunt and uncle to Mary were priceless.

After a time, the Larsons said their goodbyes, leaving Jim and Karly as the last two guests. They sat around the pool, the full moon swelling against the night sky, each nursing a snifter of brandy.

"So, Jim, tell us about your new position," Donna urged.

"There's nothing much to tell. It's basically investigative work, much the same as it was here, but a lot more of it. Speaking of investigative work, I recommended your expertise the other week, Donna." Jim was a tall, well-built man favored to become more handsome as he aged. His blond hair was showing some gray around the temples, adding a distinguished look to his warm and relaxed manner.

"You're kidding?'

"Now don't be modest. You've been building quite a reputation as a source for law enforcement to turn to for advice and consultation in stubborn cases."

"Do you have a stubborn case?" Ken inquired.

"We sure do! As you know, I replaced Russ Carotti, who retired from the Pittsburgh, Pennsylvania investigative unit. Russ handed me a folder...not really a folder, but more like a volume. Two volumes, in fact!"

"Cold cases?" Ken asked.

"Yes and no. All of the cases appear to be related. We think we have a serial killer. If we're right, he or she has been on the job for at least twenty-one years."

Donna and Ken were stunned. "Twenty-one years!" Donna exclaimed. "That's a long time not to get caught!"

"The thing is, we don't think the killings are likely to stop unless we stop them. That's where you come in, Donna."

"I'm flattered. How do you see me assisting, Jim?"

"Russ Carotti moved to The Lakes in Florida shortly after retirement. I recently spoke with him. He's offered to meet and share all he knows about the case and to answer your questions if you're agreeable to the proposition. As it turns out, he'll be back in Pittsburgh Labor Day Weekend visiting family. He suggested we meet before the weekend gets underway. If you agree, Karly and I would love to have you and Ken stay with us. Her parents are coming up that weekend as well, but we have plenty of room."

Donna turned to Karly who was nodding in agreement. "It was so good to see your parents today, Karly. They are such fun people. Your invitation is enticing and I'm already intrigued by what Jim has shared."

"I think that means we're coming to Pittsburgh, Labor Day Weekend!" Ken confirmed.

Jim and Karly met Ken and Donna at the Pittsburgh airport in the afternoon on the Thursday before Labor Day. As it turned out, Jim had arranged for Karly's parents, Jeff and Julie West, to arrive on the same flight. It was a grand welcome of family and friends.

Jim rented a large SUV for the weekend, wanting everyone to be comfortable as they toured the city. The vehicle was large enough to hold everyone's luggage without compromising the seating areas.

Jim and Karly chose a favorite Italian restaurant to have an early dinner. Jim had arranged for Donna, Ken, and himself to meet with Russ Carotti that evening, freeing up the rest of the weekend. Russ was more than agreeable, not only to the time and place, but to Ken's attendance. In the meantime, they feasted on Italian delights and wines, and the laughter never stopped. Karly's father was a comedian in his own right, with a never-ending source of jokes, stories and tales. Karly's mother, though quieter and more reserved than her husband, had her own brand of quick wit, sending a volley when you least expected it. Together, they made a great team.

With dinner over, Jim made haste, driving home to unload the luggage and show their guests to their bedrooms. Karly provided a quick tour of their home to Ken and Donna before their scheduled meeting with Russ. Luckily they didn't have far to drive, and the traffic was light.

Jim spotted Russ's car in the lighted parking lot, with Russ still sitting behind the wheel smoking a cigarette. Jim parked beside him and gave him a wave. The two exited their cars and shook hands with Ken and Donna following behind. Ken and Donna were introduced to Russ and pleasantries were exchanged before the group was led by Jim into the investigative wing of a tall, brick building, and home to Precinct 7 as well as the Investigations Division.

Many former colleagues approached to say hello, greeting Russ warmly as he and his group entered the building. Russ was a highly distinguished member of law enforcement in the Pittsburgh community, and had several scars to show for it from a shooting twenty-six years earlier. A medium-built man with a full head of gray hair, he retained a confident, warm manner.

"I take it we are headed for the Closet?" Russ asked Jim.

"Indeed, we are. Nothing has changed since you left. We still keep the door locked and only the lieutenant and I have the key."

As it turned out, the Closet was just that, but larger than most.

"We're going to have to make the best of it and just squeeze in." Jim unlocked the door and motioned for Donna and Ken to enter, with Russ and Jim following.

There was a small table in the middle of the room with one chair, and an overhead light. The walls were white painted cinder block, which helped to keep the space somewhat cool in the absence of an air vent. Taped to two of the walls were multiple photos and a large whiteboard that presented a timeline. A small shelf held both large and small folders and binders.

"Welcome to the Closet," Russ said turning to Ken and Donna. "I have spent untold hours in this room. I almost didn't retire because of this case." He had an engaging smile and manner. "I inherited this case twelve years ago from the fellow before me. We were stumped then, and we continue to be stumped. I have never been so frustrated. Retirement has allowed me to walk away from it, but not entirely. It's under my skin."

"Why don't you start from the beginning and share with Dr. DeShayne what you have shared with me, Russ?" Jim suggested.

"Gladly. At first, I thought I was looking for the murderer of one victim. As it turns out, as Jim has already told you, the twenty-one photos you see along the walls are the victims of what we believe to be a serial killer. The killings have happened all over the United States, so there is no geographic pattern. The fact a serial killer is responsible was not uncovered until about the time I took over the case."

"Twelve years ago?" Donna asked for confirmation.

"That's right." Russ replied. "Now, what's interesting is the fact there appears to be a time-related sequence."

"What do you mean?" Ken asked.

"I have been able to determine there is one killing a year, and no more."

Donna looked at the photos on the wall individually. "How do you know there are not more victims beyond these?"

"We don't know for sure, but it is our best guess right now," Jim answered for Russ.

"How were you able to determine a serial killer is responsible if the killings are all over the country?" Ken asked, ever the detective.

"As I mentioned, at the time I thought I was dealing with one victim. Interestingly, in the report of clothing and items found on the body, there was mention of a small pin, along with a photo of the item. Offhandedly, I put the info and photo of the pin in the FBI's National Crime Information Database, commonly referred to as NCID, not really expecting to get results. Bingo! I hit the 'mother lode'. The killer left a clue. The very same clue for each of the victims, twenty-one times."

"When was the last killing?" Donna asked.

Jim answered since he was now heading up the investigation. "Six months ago. An ice fisherman in Alaska had just cast his line in the lake. Before too long, he got a tug on the line and attempted to reel in his catch, pleased he had caught something so soon!

His fish turned out to be a body and the face was looking straight up! I still don't think the fisherman has recovered. I've talk to him several times since."

"Let me guess, the clothing held a pin similar to the other murders," Donna interjected.

"Not similar. An exact copy to be more correct," Jim responded.

"Do you have a photo of the pin?" Ken asked.

Jim scanned the shelf for the file he was looking for. Once found, he removed a folder, pulled out the photo and placed it on the table. Donna and Ken bent forward for a closer look. The photo revealed a gold, oval-shaped pin similar to what one might might wear on the lapel of a suit, measuring less than one-half inch in size. In the middle of the pin was an ornate rendering of a frog holding a fishing rod with bordering frond.

"This is beautifully done. Very intricate. Still, a frog? How odd. Why a frog?" Donna asked, still perusing the photo. "It seems to me if the manufacturer of the pin is found, you may find your murderer as well. Surely it can't be that hard to find the supplier for this. After all, how many frogs are designed into a pin? This must have cost a great deal to have designed and manufactured."

"Yes, one can draw that conclusion. Unfortunately, we have not been able to discover the source of the pin or what it signifies. We have even sent it to the FBI for tracking and identification, but with no success. There are no markings that indicate a manufacturer."

Donna continued to study the pin. "So it may have been privately created and produced."

"In which case we may never know the source, but it is a clue and one left by the killer," Russ added.

Donna looked at the photos on the wall, one by one. "Do we know who they are?"

"Yes, each one has been identified. Once we determined the pin was the common denominator, we were then able to establish the identities of twenty-one victims. It took a while. Months, in fact. Gathering information from all over the country proved time consuming," Russ answered.

"Are we to assume these photos are placed in the order of death?" Ken asked.

"As near as we can establish. We think we have at least ninety-five per cent accuracy," Jim shared. "The timeline we've worked out should prove helpful."

Donna and Ken took time to study the timeline on the whiteboard. "So, if I understand this correctly, the first killing was in 1994. Where?" Donna asked.

"Arizona," Russ answered.

Jim checked the timeline and then directed the group to the first photo. "This fellow, Victim One, has been identified as John Barrett Symington, born and raised in Arizona. He and his brother, James Quest Symington, were partners in the law firm, Symington and Symington in Scottsdale. For years, the cause of death was listed as a heart attack at the age of forty-seven, until the pin was discovered listed among the personal effects of the deceased years later. We've been able to construct this photo display and timeline based on this evidence."

"I wonder why the killer began in Arizona," Donna mused out loud.

"We've asked ourselves the same question, and why did the killer choose the other locations? If we can answer that, we can solve this thing," Russ projected.

"Is there any chance we can open the door wider and let in some air? It's a bit stuffy in here," Donna inquired. She had the beginnings of a headache. She was hopeful more airflow would dissipate the dampish odor and head off a full-blown headache. Jim immediately opened the door. In time, Donna felt better.

Ken was once again studying the photos and the information listed just below them. "I'm counting fourteen states, most on the eastern side of the country with the exception of Alaska and Arizona. Of these fourteen, multiple killings took place in three of them. That has to be significant."

"We think so as well," Jim agreed.

"How did this case end up here in Pittsburgh?" Ken inquired looking directly at Russ.

Russ smiled before answering. "I was wondering when you were going to ask. By accident! Or, Providence, take your pick. I attended a three-day advanced investigations convention in Atlanta in 1997. There were nearly three hundred detectives in attendance. It included roundtable discussions, and presenters from all over the United States. Seated at my table was a fellow from Arizona. We hit it off and went for dinner on the last night. We were sharing war stories and he brought up the death of our first victim, John Symington, rather offhandedly mentioning the pin among his personal affects. The family had never seen the pin before. It turns out, Symington was a distant cousin of my dinner companion so I thought nothing of it at the time, a detail of no importance, but for some unexplained reason the conversation stuck with me, all the same."

"In 2003, a body was discovered here in Pittsburgh. The case was being handled by another detective in the unit, so, again, I paid little attention until it was mentioned there was an unusual pin found on the body, a woman's body. I got curious and asked the detective about the pin. He showed a photo to me. I had kept in touch with my friend from Arizona all that time. Just out of curiosity I sent a photo of the pin to him and asked him if he was familiar with it. Turns out, it was an exact copy of the one found on the body of his cousin!"

"Wow! What are the odds of that?" Ken exclaimed.

"Exactly! It was then we decided to enter the photo of the pin into the national database. We were pretty sure the death of Mr. Symington was not related to a heart attack. It was confirmed when an autopsy was performed. The cause of death was poisoning."

Donna was still looking at each photo on the wall. "So this woman here," Donna said pointing to one, "is Victim Nine. There are three women and eighteen men."

"I take it there is no connection between the cousin of your friend from Arizona and this woman from Houston found in 2003, other than the pin," Ken surmised, directing his statement at Russ for confirmation.

"None that we have found, and believe me we have looked!" Russ countered.

"What is known about the woman?" Ken inquired.

"Not much. She was fifty years old, owned her own real estate agency, divorced eight years earlier, had two grown children, never in trouble with the law, no known enemies, a devoted church member, and she was an ardent volunteer in the Houston community."

"She sounds like a real citizen's citizen! I know I don't have to ask, but did you check out her ex-husband?" Donna asked.

"He died of a stroke months before her death. Dead end, in more ways than one."

Neither Donna nor Ken commented for a time, each reviewing the facts presented while studying the faces and the timeline.

"Let me clarify, there may be more victims. We are proceeding with the fact that twenty-one victims were found with this pin," Russ offered.

"Is there any chance I can get a copy of the timeline and the photos, Jim?" Donna asked. "I'd like to study them when I get back."

"No problem. I'll have a copy for you before you leave."

It was then Russ directed a comment at Donna. "I think we would be interested in your take from a psychological standpoint, Dr. DeShayne."

Donna's face took on a pensive look before she commented. "If indeed the murders have been a once-a-year event for the period in question, my initial response is whomever is responsible for these killings is very organized and focused. The killer devised a plan, and the plan has been executed, no pun intended, methodically and consistently all this time. My guess is the killer is highly intelligent, exacting, and very confident in his or her methodology. So confident, in fact, that the same clue is provided with each of the killings.

"Which brings us to another probability. The consistency of the same pin being found on each of the victims' bodies would indicate the killer wants these crimes to be connected by providing a clue. Whomever the killer is may believe failure on the part of law enforcement to uncover other victims as something that would upset the orderliness and preciseness of the scheme. I am fairly convinced the twenty-one found were part of a carefully contrived plan. We can only pray there are not more victims in the future."

"Do you get a sense whether we are dealing with a male or female?" Russ questioned.

"I can't help you there. Not yet, anyway. I can say with some confidence, however, the victims are not random. There is a common denominator associated with them other than the pin. Our killer has sought them out not because of location but for some other reason only the killer knows."

"We figured as much," Russ replied. "It's another missing piece of the puzzle and has frustrated me all these years."

"Jim, I can only say I'm sure there will be others, and you can only hope the killer gets careless or simply stops killing."

Chapter Five

After a hearty breakfast the next day, Jim and Karly and their houseguests set off for a tour of the city. Jim was an exceptional tour guide, dispensing to his family and friends what made Pittsburgh an attractive city in which to work and live.

"Most people know Pittsburgh as the 'Steel City' because of the Pittsburgh Steelers and the city's long history of steel manufacturing, and while that's true, Pittsburgh is also known as the City of Bridges, having more bridges than Venice, four hundred forty-six of them, in fact! Plus this town is full of museums and art collections."

"Jim and I have been enjoying the museums. We have visited several. This afternoon we are taking you to the Frick Art & Historical Center, but this morning we thought it might be nice to visit downtown," Karly added.

"Downtown is called the Golden Triangle, not only because of the confluence of the Ohio, Allegheny, and Monongahela rivers, but because it represents the land where enormous wealth was generated through the Gilded Age. Although considered the central business district, it also houses a very popular cultural district with museums and art galleries. Since more people are choosing to live in the heart of the city, it has become one grand neighborhood with lots of green space. Believe it or not, it has also overcome its one-time reputation as being a polluted industrial town and is now considered by environmentalists the second most livable city in the country!"

They arrived at the historic Market Square, considered the hub of downtown activity. Jim and Karly led Donna, Ken, and the Wests through the square, which boasted unique attractions, along with unusual boutiques. The square was teeming with activity of every sort, including a farmer's market they enjoyed strolling through. The Oyster House was decided on for lunch, a well-known downtown restaurant since 1871.

The afternoon was filled with a visit to the Frick Art & Historical Center, a cluster of museums and historical buildings with a focus on the life and times of Henry Clay Frick, a wealthy industrialist and fervent art collector during the Gilded Age of wealth creation. They would soon learn it was Helen Clay Frick, daughter of Henry Clay Frick, who doggedly determined the Frick estate be preserved and opened to the public after her death.

"I have such an interest in this time period, when a few men created wealth dynasties through their ownership in steel, railroads, oil, and banking toward the end of the nineteenth century. And a few of them realized the creation of their wealth right here in Pittsburgh," Donna said, as they strolled the eleven-room "Clayton," the former home of Henry Clay Frick and his wife, Adelaide."

The Titans of Industry," Jim returned, referring to a title often accorded the wealthy of the Gilded Age.

"Or Robber Barons," Ken added, with a hint of sarcasm.

Donna, Karly, and Julie, Karly's mother, were enthralled by the gift shop. Donna came away with a coffee-table book on the Frick Collection.

The following day, the group toured the Carnegie Museum of Art, a contemporary art museum conceived and built by Andrew Carnegie, an American industrialist whose enormous wealth was realized in Pittsburgh through steel manufacturing. Everyone was amazed at the vast collection of more than thirty thousand pieces on display, spanning almost every segment of art that included paintings and sculpture, decorative arts and design, film, video, along with prints and drawings. By the end of the day, they were spent, but exhilarated by the chance to tour the museum. Again, Donna and the ladies spent time in the gift shop, and came away with treasures to remember their visit. They headed home to grill hamburgers and spend the rest of the evening hours exchanging their comments and impressions of Pittsburgh and the museums.

"If I remember correctly," Jeff West said after a time, "Carnegie and Frick were business partners in the formation of what would eventually be known as US Steel, but later became bitter enemies."

"Two men with huge egos, I suspect," Donna posited. "Despite all that, they left a legacy of riches in their collections for the public to enjoy. I was thoroughly enthralled with the visit to both museums. Thank you, Jim and Karly, for being so thoughtful in your choice of entertainment this weekend."

"Perhaps the next time you visit, we can plan on a visit to the Phipps Conservatory and Botanical Gardens," Karly offered. "I understand it is a 'must-see' as well."

Before turning in for the night, Jim discreetly handed Donna a large binder. "I hope you have room for this in your suitcase. If not, I can mail it. It's the information you requested on the timeline and the photos."

"If I don't have room, I'm sure Ken does. I'm the one who raided the gift shops at the museums," Donna said with a hearty smile.

"I so appreciate your assistance and being another set of eyes, Donna."

"I'm honored you thought of me. I'll study it thoroughly; I can assure you."

Several days after returning from Pittsburgh, Donna met Carole for lunch at the River Towne Café, a popular restaurant they often frequented. Donna filled her friend in on the meeting with Russ Carotti, knowing Carole could keep a secret. After all, they had long shared a confidence few people knew.

Carole was leaning over the table, intently engaged in Donna's narrative. "Twenty-one killings, huh? One each year for twenty-one years! It's hard to believe such monsters exist," she responded when it was clear Donna had finished her review, "but unfortunately they do. And a frog depicted on the pin, with a fishing rod, no less! More than a little bizarre, if you ask me. So, what are you calling this guy? The Ribbet Slayer or maybe The Croaker? Hey, I think I like that one!"

Donna laughed long and hard. Carole was forever the jokester. Her sense of humor was legendary. "You really have to solve this thing," Carole went on to say. "I'll never be able to order frog legs at a restaurant again!"

"Well, don't jump to conclusions, no pun intended," Donna returned smartly, surprising herself with the unintended joke. Carole's face registered a broad smile. "This may never be solved. There is so little to go on, but I'll offer any help I can."

"Did I tell you Gavin and I are planning a trip to New York City for our twenty-fifth wedding anniversary early in December?" Carole asked, changing course. "I'd love to see New York lit up for Christmas. Oh, before I forget, Gavin wants to do Thanksgiving dinner at our place again this year. You are coming, aren't you?"

"Don't we always? Who could say no to Gavin's cooking? By the way, if you're doing New York, don't forget to schedule a visit to the Frick Museum. There is one there as well. You won't be disappointed.

Donna had been busy all morning in her office at the other end of the house when Ken came in to ask her what she wanted for lunch. It was Saturday and he had just come in from doing yard work. They had planned on a movie later that afternoon and dinner afterward.

"Whoa!" Ken remarked, eyeing the walls. "Looks like you have company," he blurted as he scanned the photos of the twenty-one victims Donna had mounted on the wall. She was about to affix the timeline and the photo of the pin when she heard his voice behind her.

"I thought it might help if I identified with the victims."

"A bit too up-close and personal for me!" he returned, placing his arm around her shoulders as she faced the wall. "Say, speaking of 'up-close and personal,'" he remarked, turning her around to enfold her into his embrace and then kiss her amorously, "how about you and I enjoy a bit of afternoon delight?"

She was breathless by the time their lips parted. "Oh, I see now. You want me to identify with *you.*"

"Something like that," Ken mumbled as he planted kisses along her neckline and behind her ear.

Donna took Ken's hand, smiling wickedly, as she led him to the bedroom. "Well, then, why don't we just have ourselves a 'get-acquainted' party?" Donna never tired of their lovemaking. Ken's body exuded a masculinity she could never resist. She loved everything about him, his towering height and commanding presence, the determination of his walk, not to mention his well-defined physique. Combined with a virile passion in his lovemaking that never failed to propel Donna toward heightened anticipation and joyous fulfillment, she surrendered as a more than willing and able participant.

Working in her home office the next afternoon, Donna pondered the photos on the wall and decided to focus on isolating the victims slain in the same state. Of the fourteen states representing the crime scenes, there were seven victims sharing the same state with another victim. Of the seven, Pennsylvania had three victims, New York had two, and Ohio had two. Of the three in Pennsylvania, one was a woman. She then turned her attention to listing the ages of each of the victims. All were between forty and fifty years old. She questioned the significance of this. Why did the killer not target someone younger or older than this age group?

Reviewing the reports on each of the victims, she found all of them had been poisoned. Many, at first, as in the case of Mr. Symington, were thought to have died of a heart attack. Donna noted the killer made use of several types of poisons. Could this mean the killer had a medical background, perhaps pharmacology, or even biology? Donna then listed the profession or occupation of each of the victims. Each of them was a high earning professional, all having a respected presence in law, medicine, real estate, or industry. All were churchgoers, and all contributed to community efforts through generous donations to local causes. None had been in trouble with the law.

She was beginning to understand Russ Carotti's frustration. There was a thread of similarity among the victims, namely age, income, and a respected presence in their communities, both professionally and through various charitable outlets. Then there was the pin. She decided to call Jim Callahan.

"It's great to hear from you, Donna, although I didn't expect to hear from you so soon."

"I've been sorting my way through the details in the files you gave me. I've got a couple of questions. Do you have a minute?"

"I've got all the time you need."

Donna then shared her findings on the similarity of the victims.

"Impressive!" he exclaimed when she finished her narrative. "We knew they were all professionals, but didn't catch the age thing. I admit I'm not one hundred percent up to speed."

"Here's my question, though. While I understand the murders took place in various locations, didn't at least one medical examiner question the cause of death?"

"Apparently not. Russ Carotti has a theory on this, one that I am inclined to agree with. The victims, being well-known in their communities, had private physicians. The medical examiner would be inclined to accept the findings of the private physician. No autopsy was performed on any of the victims until we raised the possibility of foul play, and again, no toxicology screen was ordered, all assuming the cause of death was heart related.

"The thing to remember is many medical examiners are under budget restraints. If murder is not suspected, there is no reason to go further. Mindful of having to justify the annual budget, the average medical examiner would prefer to take the easy way out. In these cases, nothing was suspicious at first blush."

"You mentioned toxicology screening. Are they not required to order, at least, that test?" Donna probed.

"Again, they relied on the physician's statement. However, a poison can be used that is not readily detectable in most drug screens. On the other hand, should a toxicology report show positive for poisoning, it will not necessarily reveal which one, given that many poisons break down into different chemicals over time. To determine the source or type of the poison requires more expensive and time-consuming testing; a road most MEs would rather not go down in consideration of their budgets."

"Are all poisons on the typical screening?" Donna asked.

"Now that's another point. The answer is no."

"So the killer may have used a substance not found on the typical screening"

"Yes."

Donna tried to wrap her head around Jim's summary. "Should I assume because each of the twenty-one victims was well-known and respected, it propelled a deeper probe into the cause of death?"

"Once the families understood their loved ones were murdered, they most likely insisted on a detailed report."

"They had the political pull?" Donna questioned.

"Most likely."

"Even the early bodies were exhumed and tested?"

"For the most part. Three of the bodies were embalmed. Embalming can severely impede toxicology reports."

"So I assume you moved forward on those based on the presence of the pin?"

"That's correct. The others were buried without having been embalmed. Keep in mind, an intact corpse can reveal a staggering amount of information, even years after death. It is possible to obtain a chemical fingerprint for any molecule, so every compound can be distinguished from every other one and isolated."

"I noticed in my review the killer would change up the poisons, never using the same one from the previous killing until several killings later. I wonder why?" Donna questioned, thinking out loud.

"Russ and I discussed this as well. Russ thinks it was to avoid suspicion from the supplier."

"Hmmm. It could be, but I'm not convinced. What can you tell me about the poisons used? I see methanol was used more than the others."

"That's probably because methanol is highly toxic, colorless, odorless, and tasteless. Its effects often mimic respiratory or heart failure after being ingested twelve to twenty-four hours earlier. The victim would need treatment two hours after ingestion to be saved."

"What about the other poisons?" Donna inquired.

"One of the others was aconite. The symptoms of aconite poisoning usually takes place within ten to twenty minutes of ingestion and are often mistaken for cardiac arrest. Then the use of tetrodotoxin was evident in some cases. Most people associate TTX with the pufferfish. Extremely toxic, it can be administered by ingestion, injection, inhalation, or through a simple break in the skin. Generally, the cause of death is attributed to severe respiratory failure."

"So death in the use of these poisons comes quickly."

"Relatively quickly, yes. The killer would have to administer enough of the poison to affect a quick death. That kind of information can be found online, if one is diligent in their search."

"Or the killer could have a background in chemistry."

"Yes, that may be the case."

"By the way," Donna interjected, hoping to add some humor to a serious conversation, "Carole Tandermann suggests we should call our killer The Ribbet Slayer or The Croaker. What do you think?"

Jim laughed before answering. "That sounds like something Carole would suggest. I take it she saw a photo of the pin. In that case, between us, let's call the killer the Croaker."

Chapter Six

He'd thought about it for years. Devising and executing a plan was another story. It was only recently he had information that propelled him toward escape. After sixteen years in prison, freedom would be a welcome change. He wasn't going to get caught. Never again. Once on the outside he had a job to do, and wouldn't rest until it was accomplished. His hatred had only grown in prison, his mind turning over and over again the details of his arrest and trial. Betrayal was not something that set well with him. All these years every cell in his body harbored a festering boil of malice. It was time to set it free.

His connections on the outside had dissipated through the years. There were still one or two he could count on. Once out he would recreate himself. He had learned a great deal in prison, always listening but never giving a hint of himself or his past. Other inmates stayed away from him, knowing him to be dangerous and volatile. He was without conscience, the worst kind.

A new inmate gave him his first break. The inmate was disgustingly obese, and scared out of his mind. He had reason to be. Prison was not for the faint of heart, especially for one so unprepared. The new prisoner came to him for protection. It was the first thing you learned in prison, but you had to have collateral, something to trade: sex, money, drugs, information, or a useful connection. What could the fat slob possibly have to insure his own safety?

The fat man was highly alert and noticed something that might prove useful. There was a photo in the Protector's cell. He knew who it was; he traded information about what he knew of the person in the frame. The new inmate not only got protection, he was shown favor in other ways. Food was a favorite.

The planned escape was never discussed with the rotund man. Once the breakout was complete, the chubby would be on his own, void of protection. Heaven help him. He would be thrown to the wolves, and the wolves were vicious and hungry.

Gavin had been in the kitchen since the early morning, preparing the Thanksgiving feast. Carole's only assignment was to make the coffee. Carole was not offended. Everyone, including she, agreed she was lousy in the kitchen.

Their guests were already arriving for the midday dinner. Saul, Lacy Sue, and Mary Larson were the first to arrive. Lacy Sue was very pregnant, with less than six weeks until her due date. They were to have twins! Lacy Sue headed straight for the kitchen to assist Gavin, leaving Saul and Mary to set the table. Before long, Donna and Ken, Jim and Karly, Jeff and Julie West, and Caleb and Sienna Blackwell, along with their two young sons, Paul and Samuel, arrived bearing their culinary contributions to the buffet table. The children ran out to the backyard to play, the weather being sunny and somewhat cool, but not cold.

Just as the buffet table was ready, the doorbell rang. Gavin and Carole glanced at each other with a knowing look. "Ken, why don't you get the door, while I carve the turkey?" Gavin suggested.

"Sure," Ken said, placing his wine glass on the table before heading to the front door. The group waited for the door to open and for the reunion to begin. They were all in on it, except for Donna.

"Well, just don't stand there, Daddy," Megan Daniels Bishop said. Her dad was caught off guard, completely surprised by the sight of his daughter and son-in-law, Greg, and Greg's parents, Rick and Catherine Bishop. "Either give us a hug, or let us in!"

Ken immediately drew his daughter in for an emotional embrace. In the meantime, the group gathered by the door, pleased with themselves for orchestrating this surprise. Donna's face registered complete delight and she moved past Ken to hug Megan and her husband and his parents.

"You didn't know?" Ken asked Donna, tears dancing on his eyelashes after greeting the new arrivals.

"No! Apparently I was kept in the dark as well," Donna replied, looking over her shoulder at Gavin and Carole, who looked pleased with themselves.

"We love it when a plan comes together!" Carole boomed. The rest of the group applauded.

It took a while for everyone to settle down, all talking at once. Ken blew his nose on more than one occasion, still moved by the surprise. Donna went to stand with him, embracing him around the waist before looking up into his eyes. "I wish it were my idea."

At that he teared up again. "My two most beautiful and precious women in the same room! I am a lucky man!"

The children were called in, the food put out, and the feasting began. The buffet table boasted of culinary delights of every description, prepared to perfection. The wine flowed freely, the laughter was endless, and memories were made once again.

At last, Gavin presented the desserts, assigning them to their own table. He regaled his guests with selections of confection, cakes, pies, and cookies that brought *ohs* and *ahs*. Carole produced three Keurig brewers along with top-of-the-line K-cups of coffees, teas, and hot chocolates of every description and flavor. For hours, it was an endless gastronomical delight.

Eventually board and card games were brought out for the women, while the men ventured into the den to watch football. The children went back outside to play until it got dark. The fireplace was casting its warmth and glow, creating a cozy atmosphere.

When the football game was over, there was another visit to the dessert table. After-dinner drinks were offered and being enjoyed when Megan tapped the side of her glass to get the groups attention.

"First of all, Greg and I want to thank Gavin and Carole for their generosity this day. In the spirit of Thanksgiving, and every other day, I think we can all toast to our many blessings, but especially to the friendship of these two dear and loving people, who once again brought us all together as friends and family." The clinking of glassware could be heard along with a round of applause. "Another reason for gratitude," Megan continued, "is that our circle of friends and family is growing, in more ways than one!" Megan looked at Lacy Sue and smiled. Everyone laughed. Lacy Sue blushed. Saul put his arms around his wife and daughter's shoulder, looking every bit the proud husband and father.

"We're having twins!" Mary called out loudly.

"They are lucky to have a big sister like you, Mary!" Megan returned. Again, the group applauded. Mary looked so proud. Gavin and Carole melted at the sight of her beaming face. "Greg and I have one more blessing to share. Dad, Donna, Rick, and Catherine are to be grandparents. We are three months pregnant!"

It was pandemonium. Everyone rose from their seats or stepped forward to congratulate the couple. Ken was teary again. Rick and Catherine hugged each other, thrilled with the news.

"Have you had a sonogram? Is it a boy or a girl?" Mary managed to yell above the din of the gathering.

"How does this child know these things?" Carole asked Gavin, their eyes watching their granddaughter's every expression while enjoying the jubilation around them.

"Don't forget, her mother is a nurse *and* pregnant! I'm sure Mary has been asking enough questions to be exhausting!"

"When I was young, they didn't have this sort of thing. I remember when I first heard the term sonogram. I thought it was a singing telegram when a son was born. I began to wonder why I never heard of a girl-o-gram!"

Gavin roared with laughter, giving his wife a kiss. "You may not be able to cook, but you sure know how to tickle my funny bone."

"I'd like to tickle more than your funny bone, big guy!" she returned with a mischievous wink.

The second week in December found the Tandermanns touring New York City in celebration of their twenty-fifth wedding anniversary. It had been a long time since they'd visited the city, not since their relocation from New Jersey to South Carolina years ago. The festive offerings of the city enthralled them. From Rockefeller Center's world-renowned lighted Christmas tree along with ice skating at Bryant Park, to Radio City Music Hall for a performance by the Rockettes, to the enchanting holiday window displays along Fifth Avenue, the days were filled with the kind of starry-eyed wonder often reserved for children. They even visited the Frick Museum, the Ground Zero Museum, and Ellis Island. They slept late, partied late, and made love like they were on their honeymoon. Their favorite dining experience was Barbetta's, an Italian restaurant in the theater district frequented by the famous and informed. It was an unexpected gift card given to them at the Myrtle Beach airport by Donna and Ken as well as Saul, Lacy Sue, and Mary.

Toward the end of their stay, they happened upon a fairly large used bookstore, craft shop, and consignment store. Many of the items offered were made by hand with some of the proceeds going to charity. They purchased several items as Christmas presents. The back of the shop hosted used books, magazines, and comics of every description. Gavin was an avid reader of sci-fi, not to mention cookbooks. The place was haphazardly put together with no real order. Most of the books were stuffed in plastic crates, with crate piled upon crate. One had to be willing to move them to explore their contents. That was fine with Gavin. He was in heaven.

Carole took up a station at the other end of the store in the consignment area looking for Occupied Japan pieces. She had been collecting these mementos for years and had nearly one hundred in her collection. It was not that the collection was stunning, in fact, most of Occupied Japan pieces were sold as cheap souvenirs in their day at the end of World War II. It was the stamp on the bottom of the souvenir, Made in Occupied Japan, that made them collectible. From her research, she knew during the Allied occupation of Japan for a seven-year period after the war, from 1945-1952, fifty percent of all Japanese exports were required to be stamped either "Occupied Japan" or "Made in Occupied Japan." At one point after the Allies left the country, it is reported the Japanese government found the stamp to be an affront and sent out teams around the world to find and destroy any item with a stamp or tag. She enjoyed 'the hunt' as Gavin would say.

They had been scavenging for nearly an hour when Carole moved toward the back of the store where Gavin was still rooting through boxes and crates. She discovered a wooden crate crammed full of magazines and brochures, some quite dated and out-of-print. To her delight, she found old *Life* magazines, along with museum and travel literature. Carole called to Gavin when she discovered an old *Omni* sci-fi magazine and a *Twilight Zone* magazine. He joined her, already having a stack of finds in his hands. Reaching down toward the bottom of the crate, she unearthed a very old book featuring Andrew Carnegie on the front cover. Examining it more closely, Carole concluded it was an old biography of the man. It wasn't unusual for the very wealthy to hire a biographer to write and catalogue their life story with photos. Normally, she wouldn't have shown any interest in the find if it weren't for the fact Donna had excitedly shared information about her visit to the Carnegie Museum of Art while in Pittsburgh. She casually flipped through the pages, which amounted to an overview of the man's life, his accomplishments, and charitable giving. She was about to put the periodical back when a photo caught her eye. It was a group picture, with Andrew Carnegie taking a prominent place in the front row alongside Henry Clay Frick. Her eyes were drawn, not to the group of faces staring back, but to an item hanging on the wall behind them.

"Gavin, I have got to have this book!" she fairly yelled.

"So you shall, my dear, but why all the excitement?"

"Look!" she said, showing the photo to him."

"It's an old photograph. Why all the interest?"

"Donna is going to love this!" Carole, with an air of determination, headed straight to the register to purchase her find, leaving Gavin shaking his head.

Several days after arriving home from New York, Carole and Donna met for lunch.

"Tell me about New York," Donna said as they seated themselves.

"That can wait! I found something!" Carole said excitedly.

Donna looked at her friend quizzically.

"Here!" Carole said, abruptly handing the find from New York to her friend. "Merry Christmas!"

Donna reached across the table to take the book from Carole. "Thank you, I think. Is this a joke?" All Donna saw was a stained and shabby memoir with a photo of Andrew Carnegie on the cover.

"No, this is not a joke! You can nominate your best friend to the Hall of Friends at any point after this!" Carole returned conspiratorially. "Look on page twenty-eight!"

Donna immediately turned to page twenty-eight while struggling to keep some of the more deteriorated pages of the book from falling out. She studied the photo. "This is a group picture. Very nice, but I don't see what all the excitement is about."

"That's because you haven't really looked at it. Try again, girlfriend, because I'm not going to let you order lunch until you hit the jackpot."

Donna knew Carole would be true to her word. She had already shooed away the waitress. She turned her attention back to the photo.

"Okay, the caption says, 'Andrew Carnegie, front row, fifth from left, with lodge members, South Creek Fishing and Hunting Club, Pittsburgh, Pennsylvania, 1885.' Not too inspiring, if you ask me." It was then she brought the book closer and spotted what Carole had seen. "Oh, my God! It can't be!" Donna yelled, half out of her seat, drawing the attention of the other diners.

Carole grinned while summoning the waitress. "Miss, we're ready to order now."

Chapter Seven

The prisoner had arranged to be reassigned to the laundry. It had taken little time to win the confidence of the guards. Periodic transfers of money into bank accounts solidified alliances. Money was the great equalizer. Most of the guards had money problems, or at the very least, a thirst for money. There were no secrets in prison, only opportunities. Information was power. Power was what he was all about. He had established his power base early on. It was a move straight out of the play book of mobster Charles "Lucky" Luciano when imprisoned in 1936. Lucky was his hero. The prisoner had studied the infamous Mafia boss and head of the Commission, a governing body created by Luciano for organized crime, and knew Luciano not only ran his vast empire from Sing Sing Correctional Facility in New York, but also ran the prison as well. It was the prisoner's intent to pattern his confinement after the legendary Lucky Luciano, even down to his work assignment in the laundry and having a personal chef prepare his meals.

He studied the weaknesses and knew the laundry truck visited the outbuildings in the vicinity of the prison, dropping off clean sheets and clothing every two weeks. A few of the upper tier prison officials and guards lived on site in these outbuildings, referred to as "cottages." The laundry truck was the Achilles heel. Discreet inquiries and transfers of money gave him all the information he needed. For six months, he worked out the details of his escape, keeping the photo that provided such relished information from the fat man in plain view. It was a photo he despised, the bane of his existence. It represented unforgivable betrayal. The person staring back had to be expunged, and he had to do it himself. There would be no sense of satisfaction in assigning a hit man to the task. He needed to see the fear, hear the pleas for forgiveness and mercy, watch the crying and the begging, and witness the final gasping breath leave the body. He wanted total control, and would have it.

"Did you get my fax?" Donna asked Jim the very next day after receiving the tattered book from Carole. She had faxed a copy of the photo to him the moment she got back to her office. They arranged for a time to talk.

"Yes, I did. This is a lucky break for sure. I haven't had time to research the time period. I intend to do that later today."

"Well, I have!"

"I'm not surprised. The one thing I admire about you is your tenacity."

Donna chuckled. "Ken says I'm of the Pit Bull breed. Once I clamp down, I don't let go."

"I have to agree with him. Fortunately, you don't have the face of a Pit Bull," Jim said jovially. "What have you found?"

"I thought you would never ask. I believe the photo is of some of the members of an exclusive lodge created in 1879 for wealthy industrialists and financiers, called the South Fork Fishing and Hunting Club, on the Lake Conemaugh reservoir less than a two-hour drive from Pittsburgh. In all, there were sixty-one members, including Andrew Carnegie and Henry Clay Frick, as shown in the photo, but other members included Andrew Mellon and Philander Knox."

"They were all heavy hitters in their day."

"Yes, very wealthy and influential men who operated an exclusive and secretive retreat near South Fork, Pennsylvania. The interesting thing, however, is the wall hanging behind the group."

"What are the odds of finding a photo depicting the pin found on our murder victims? An incredible piece of good fortune. The photo states it was taken in Pittsburgh? Why not Lake Conemaugh?"

"I suspect a misprint, but we can thank Carole for finding the photo. The good news continues. You can tour the South Fork Clubhouse. The National Park Service has jurisdiction over the lodge at the Johnstown Flood National Memorial and gives free tours."

"Then let's do it. Somewhere in here there's a story."

Jim had arranged a private tour of the South Fork Hunting and Fishing Club shortly after New Year's. The lodge was closed during the winter months, but when Jim explained the visit was part of a murder investigation, the Park Service provided a private showing. Jim suggested to Donna and Ken they make it a couple's weekend.

Jim and Karly met Donna and Ken at the Pittsburgh Airport two days after New Year's. They then headed for Johnstown, Pennsylvania to stay at the Heiser House, a bed and breakfast on the far end of town. Donna was glad Karly reminded them to dress warmly. Snow had already blanketed the region and the temperature was hovering just above thirty-two degrees when they arrived at the inn. It was located in a beautiful setting. This five-bedroom home was draped in exquisite Victorian detail, complete with a wraparound porch that greeted them upon arrival. The stately trees and grounds, though covered in snow, still held the decorations from Christmas, creating an enchanting winter wonderland effect.

A fire was ablaze in the large living room as the inn's owner, George Heiser, welcomed them enthusiastically when they entered. Heiser was a short man who combed his hair across his head to hide the fact he was bald. He was pudgy in a Pillsbury Doughboy kind of way, his manner warm and engaging.

"This is a beautiful home, Mr. Heiser," Donna commented as she looked about the stately surroundings.

"Thank you. Please, call me George. This home has been in the family for years. Much of it is original and some of it restored. It's a constant project, but I love it. Fortunately, I have help with the grounds in the summer, and assistance with the cooking and cleaning throughout the year. I was pleased I could accommodate you this weekend. This is usually a busy time of year for us with skiers coming in. What brings you to our neck of the woods? You don't appear to be skiers."

Jim answered, careful not to reveal too much. "We decided to do a couple's weekend after managing to get a private tour of the South Fork Clubhouse tomorrow morning."

George Heiser looked puzzled. "South Fork Clubhouse, you say? That's closed during the winter. How did you manage that?"

"Connections," is all Jim said in return.

"I'll say. Connections would be the only way to get them to open the place before April. Well, let me show you to your rooms."

After settling in, they returned to the living room to enjoy a complimentary glass of wine and cheese tray in front of the fireplace before heading out for dinner. Breakfast the next morning was scrumptious and varied, presented on a sideboard in the breakfast room, a beautiful glass enclosure off the living room overlooking a large pond and heavily treed area behind it. It had snowed again during the night; the tree limbs bore a layer of white, as the morning sun glistened in silent greeting. The effect was beautiful!

Finishing their breakfast, the couples headed for the Visitor Center at the Johnstown National Memorial. There, they were met by Ranger Erin Summers, a light-haired, wiry woman not more than thirty years old in a National Parks Service uniform and winter wear.

"We so appreciate you accommodating our request, Ranger," Jim said after introducing the group while presenting his business card and credentials.

"To tell you the truth, Detective, it gets pretty boring up here this time of year, so I'm grateful for the change in routine. Why the interest in the clubhouse, if I may ask?"

Jim produced a photo of the pin and showed it to the park ranger, avoiding any mention of the murders. "Does this look familiar?"

"Why, yes, it does! I'll show you why when we get to the clubhouse."

At Ranger Summers' suggestion, they drove to the clubhouse in the ranger's vehicle, which was large enough for the five of them and equipped to handle the snow-filled and winding roads. Once there, she led them to the clubhouse and unlocked the door. The three-story building must have been imposing in its day, but now bore signs of neglect. Their guide told them that through the years the property had gone through several changes in ownership until recently coming under the jurisdiction of the National Park Service, whose plan is to restore it to near original condition.

"The South Fork Fishing and Hunting Club owned the Western Reservoir, the dam that created the reservoir, and one hundred-sixty acres of land surrounding it. Club members built a forty-seven-room building along with sixteen privately-owned cottages along the shoreline of the lake. The Western Reservoir was renamed Lake Conemaugh. For its day, it was a spectacular presentation."

"Wow!" Karly said, fully engrossed in the tour.

"It's in desperate need of restoration, but fortunately there's a great deal of enthusiasm toward the project. Every effort will be made to retain the wood grain floors and the original colors on the walls. As you can see, the twelve-foot-high ceramic tiled fireplace still remains and is in relatively good shape. I wish I could take you to see one of the few remaining cottages on the lake's shore, but they are slated for renovation and closed. When the repairs are complete, I anticipate they will be included in the tour as well.

"The club had a fleet of boats, including two steam yachts, numerous sailboats and canoes, and a boathouse for storage. For entertainment, there was an annual regatta, musical performances through the summer as well as various forms of theatre. It truly was a place for the very wealthy. However, I think your interest lies in the dining room. Follow me."

Ranger Summers led them to a nearby room that had once served as the dining room. It could seat one hundred and fifty guests in its day. Various photos lined the walls, depicting many of the members holding their hunting or fishing accomplishments in a proud pose.

"I think this is what you are interested in," the ranger offered, pointing to a hanging. On the far wall, she pointed out the official seal of the club. Donna and Jim walked over to have a closer look. It was round, about two feet in diameter, the outer edges made of a dark bronze. The smaller, inner gold layer bore the imprint "South Fork Fishing and Hunting Club–1879." Within the sphere was an artist rendering of a frog sitting before a pond on a mushroom cap, holding a fishing rod. It was very similar to the pin!

"Would you know if club members were issued pins like the one shown to you earlier?" Donna asked Ranger Summers.

"Like a lapel pin? That would be a question for the curator of the Johnstown Flood Museum, but I wouldn't be surprised. Money was no object for this group," said Ranger Summers.

Ken and Karly came up behind the three others to have a look at the clubhouse seal.

"It seems this seal is rather understated given the vast wealth of the members. Carnegie and Frick, at least, were avid collectors of art and sculpture. They had a taste for the exquisite. This seal is almost comical," Donna said to no one in particular.

"It could be an example of why this place may have been a welcome departure from their usual opulent lifestyles, a kind of 'roughing it,'" Karly offered. Turning to Ranger Summers, Karly asked, "How long did the club exist?"

"Only ten years. The land and dam were purchased in 1879 by Mr. Benjamin Ruff, a railroad tunnel contractor and real estate broker from Pittsburgh. It was Mr. Ruff who conceived the idea of an exclusive lodge at the South Fork dam and convinced his good friend, Henry Clay Frick, to join the club. Once Frick did so, he became a promoter and spokesman for the club, drawing other wealthy benefactors such as Carnegie, Mellon, Daniel Morrell, and numerous other powerful industrialist and businessmen to become members. Ruff remained president until his death in 1887, at which point Colonel Elias Unger became its second president until the dam broke in May 1889, causing the Johnstown Flood."

"What happened to the club then?" Ken asked.

"It closed. Many viewed lodge members as being responsible for the Johnstown Flood. Others viewed the group, especially Carnegie, as a hero for relief efforts after the catastrophe. Many of your questions can be answered by a visit to the Johnstown Flood Museum. If you haven't already been there, it can be a great resource."

"Oh, we passed it on the way in last night!" Donna returned. "I think we should tour it while we are here. Good idea!"

"This has been very insightful, Ranger Summers. We'll have lunch and tour the museum this afternoon. Is there anyone we can speak with while we are there?" Jim asked.

"Yes, that would be the curator, Thea Germaine. Let me call her to let her know you'll be coming in this afternoon." As Ranger Summers stepped away to make the call, the group wandered about. Ken and Donna continued to examine the photos in the dining room, while Jim and Karly went back to the living room to have another look.

"This was a secretive place where the powerful met to make deals and influence outcomes. I can picture them sitting around in overstuffed leather chairs, smoking the finest Cuban cigars, drinking the most expensive brandy or cognac, with conquest and self-satisfaction written all over their faces, bragging about their accomplishments," Donna said to Ken as they reviewed the photos.

"The kind of wealth we are talking about makes all the rules," Ken replied.

"Yet, their contributions in the form of art, sculpture, libraries, and institutions of learning, while serving as benefactors to a whole host of social issues, can't be ignored either. There is always the flip side of the coin."

Before long Ranger Summers joined Donna and Ken. "You're all set. Thea Germaine will be in all afternoon. Just ask for her at the front desk."

Once back at the Visitor Center, each one gathered around Ranger Summers to offer their words of appreciation for her time and effort. They promised to return again in the summer when the park offered a ranger-supervised van tour following the path of the Johnstown Flood of 1889. With a recommendation from her for a place to stop for lunch, they headed back to Johnstown.

By early afternoon, Jim found parking at the Johnstown Flood Museum. The building itself had originally been a library, a donation by Andrew Carnegie, after the flood. They would learn Carnegie donated heavily to the creation of libraries, both public and university-connected institutions. In all, more than twenty-five hundred libraries were the results of Carnegie's donations from 1883 to 1929, both in the United States and abroad.

The museum itself was an imposing three-story structure encased in light-colored brick with a slate roof complete with architectural complements so common for the day. Originally built at a cost of fifty thousand dollars, the library was converted to the Johnstown Flood Museum in 1973 when the library was moved two blocks away. Upon entering the foyer, the welcome desk was to the right and a small gift center was to the left with prominently displayed books written on the subject of the flood, along with other items of interest.

After paying the entry fee, it took the couples well over an hour to make their way through the museum, so engrossed were they with the exhibits and displays. After a time, Jim and Donna went back to the front desk to see whether the curator, Thea Germaine, still had time to meet with them. Ken and Karly agreed to continue with the exhibits and displays. Within minutes, a dignified middle-aged woman in striking attire came across the foyer, approaching Donna and Jim with her hand extended.

"I'm Thea Germaine. Welcome to our museum and city," she said, greeting them warmly. "I understand you have some questions for me. Why don't we go back to my office so we can talk?"

Leading Jim and Donna down several hallways, they entered a well-appointed office with colorful drapery and a commanding desk rumored to have once been owned by the second president of the South Fork Fishing and Hunting Club, Colonel Elias

Unger. Against the far wall was a beautifully scrolled wooden table bearing an elegant display of various photos of Thea Germaine poised with well-known dignitaries and entertainers who had visited the museum, or who had made contributions to the museum's foundation.

"Oh, I see someone borrowed one of my chairs. Excuse me while I find one." Shortly she returned to her office followed by a man carrying a chair.

"Thank you, Bob," she said when the man placed the chair beside the one already there. Addressing Jim and Donna, Ms. Germaine continued. "Jim and Donna, I would like you to meet Bob Boykin. Bob is our go-to-guy when something needs fixing around here. We don't know what we would do without him."

The maintenance man was small in stature with a receding hairline. He appeared to be in his middle sixties. His manner was reserved, almost shy, not really looking at Donna and Ken until he shook their hand. Once he left the room, Jim and Donna sat down.

"Now, how can I help you?" Thea Germaine asked as she sat behind her desk. "I understand you've been up to the clubhouse."

"We have," Jim affirmed. "It is a fascinating place, as well as this museum."

"We've made every effort to preserve our history, as tragic as it once was."

Careful not to reveal too much, Jim pulled out the photo of the pin and handed it to the curator. "We are interested in knowing the source of this pin."

Thea looked it over carefully, examining the images of both sides. "I've never seen one of these before. Where did you get it?"

"I'm not at liberty to share that information with you just yet, but it is important this conversation be kept highly confidential."

"I understand. Rest assured, nothing said here will leave this office. You have seen the clubhouse seal then?"

"Yes, we have. The similarity between the pin and the seal is intriguing. Is there any chance the pin was given to each member of the lodge?" Jim asked.

"I'm afraid I'm not going to be much help to you. I simply don't know the answer. Most of the records of the South Fork Club were lost when the firm representing the lodge, especially after the flood, threw out a bunch of papers in 1917 when moving to a newer building. It's possible the answer to your questions were in those papers."

Donna leaned forward in her chair. "So, if I understand the timeline from our tour of the clubhouse, the South Fork Club was formed ten years before the dam broke, but did not continue to operate after the flood?"

"No, it did not. It closed shortly thereafter and the corporation that was formed upon the club's creation disbanded in 1904. As you may have surmised by some of our presentations, the club was vilified in the press, the members blamed for inadequate upkeep of the seventy-two-foot-high dam."

"Why was that?" Donna inquired.

"When the club took ownership ten years previously, they made minor repairs and enlarged the lake as well. In the process, they removed three cast iron discharge pipes, which had allowed for the release of water. Without them, there was no way to drain the lake or repair the dam properly. The winter of 1888 was particularly wet. Adding to wet winter conditions, there were unprecedented rains beginning on May 30th. The water table of the South Fork Dam was rising at a rate of one inch every ten minutes. Some effort was made to contain the water, but it was fruitless. When the dam broke at 2:55 the afternoon of May 31st, twenty million gallons of water careened through the valley at speeds as high as forty miles per hour, taking everything in its path. The flood struck several other communities before reaching Johnstown in just under an hour's time. More than twenty-two hundred people were killed that day."

"Didn't *anyone* sound a warning about the dam being weakened?" Donna asked, shocked by the curator's summary.

"This is where it gets interesting. It is suspected Daniel Morrell, general manager of the Cambria Iron Company of Johnstown, bought membership into the retreat to keep a close eye on the group shortly after the club's formation. You see, Cambria Iron was heavily invested in Johnstown, and Morrell was curious as to what this group was all about. He took it upon himself to have his own engineer examine the dam. The engineer returned a report to Morrell outlining grave concern over the removal of the discharge pipes, the substandard repairs, and the potential for disaster.

"Morrell forwarded a letter as well as the engineer's report to Benjamin Ruff, the founder of the retreat and urged an overhaul of the dam. Ruff rejected Morrell's concern, insisting there was no need for alarm. Morrell died almost four years before the Johnstown Flood. Benjamin Ruff died nearly two years before the flood. This is probably more than you wanted to know, but I have always found it interesting these two highly-influential men never faced the consequences of their opposing positions regarding the safety of the dam.

"I regret I haven't been able to help you isolate the history of the pin, however. You came all this way for nothing. Perhaps it is a fluke, a coincidence the pin and South Fork seal are so similar," Thea concluded.

"Perhaps, but we had to follow through nonetheless," Jim replied.

"By the way, where are you staying?" Thea asked.

"The Heiser House," Donna answered.

"Isn't it lovely? George Heiser is our biggest supporter. Each year he hosts a fundraising benefit at his B & B for the museum. It's quite the event. Black tie, horse drawn carriages, the works. People come from miles around to attend. George makes sure they bring their checkbooks!"

"That must be fun! He maintains such a beautiful property. What did he do for a living?"

"George inherited a great deal of old family money. His great-grandfather, Victor Heiser, who was sixteen years-old at the time of the flood, lost both his parents to the waters and eventually left Johnstown. He later became a physician, spending his entire life combating disease around the world. He is best known for discovering a cure for leprosy. Victor Heiser left behind substantial means. The family invested wisely through the years. George is an only child and inherited the family fortune. So George travels, collects art, and graces us with his spirited support of our community."

Jim and Donna thanked Thea for her time and found Ken and Karly in the gift shop. Donna purchased several books on the Johnstown Flood before they left for the afternoon's wine and cheese offering at the Heiser House.

George Heiser was just setting out a fruit and cheese platter as they entered.

"Just in time!" he announced. "How was your visit to the clubhouse?"

"Fascinating!" Donna replied, noting the platter's pleasing presentation. "We went to the museum afterward and spoke with

Thea Germaine. She couldn't have been more gracious with her time. She speaks very highly of you."

"Thea is a grand lady. She has done a wonderful job promoting the museum as well as the arts in Johnstown."

The four settled in the comfortable seating in the living room as George handed each a glass of wine. The fireplace was roaring, creating an inviting warmth.

"She tells us you are a very strong supporter of the museum as well," Jim contributed.

"Oh, she must be referring to the fundraising benefit we hold each year here on the property. Say, you might think about attending this year. It's held every May on the anniversary of the flood. I warn you, we are unabashed when it comes to asking for donations," George said with a mischievous grin at the couples

Ken looked at Donna. "What do you think?"

"I think I love the idea! It's such a pretty time of year with everything in bloom."

"The property is especially beautiful at that point in the season, thanks to my groundskeeper." George continued. "I have four rooms here at the inn if you choose to book now. I offer a discounted rate for the occasion."

"Oh, Carole and Gavin would love this as well," Donna commented to Ken. "Perhaps we can invite them and the Wests. Let's book for all of us while the rooms are available."

"Then count us all in," Jim returned, getting a nod from Karly.

"The National Flood Memorial at South Fork will be fully opened by then. You may want to visit it while you're here, as well as the Grandview Cemetery where seven hundred seventy-seven small white marble headstones are laid out in precise order to commemorate the flood's unknown dead. It's quite a sight."

"A splendid idea, George!" Donna said. "I have a leaning toward significant historical events. Up until now, the Johnstown Flood had escaped my notice."

Chapter Eight

The anticipated phone call finally came. Lacy Sue Sellers was in labor! Carole and Gavin went into grandparent mode, signing Mary out of school mid-morning, while Saul paced at the hospital in the obstetrics ward. The plan was to gather Mary and meet at the hospital so the little girl could witness the birth of her two new siblings, and they definitely wanted Carole and Gavin present as well. It was to be a family affair!

Mary was all aglow as she witnessed the activity in the birthing room. The doctor and nurses were all busy, taking charge of her mother. Soon she heard a whimper and then a cry! It was a girl! Minutes later, another cry, more like a wail! It was a boy! It was an event she would never forget. Dressed in blue and pink blankets, both newborns were presented to their parents shortly after birth. Lacy Sue and Saul cried at the sight of their healthy newborns.

"Why are Mommy and Daddy crying?" Mary asked of Carole and Gavin.

"Oh, Mary! Their tears are joyful ones. The birth of children is a happy time," Carole explained.

"Oh! What will we name them?" Mary asked inquisitively.

The room fell quiet, all looking upon the cherubic faces of the newborns. Finally, a voice spoke. "Saul and I wish them to be named Carole and Gavin Larson," Lacy Sue pronounced confidently from her bed.

The escape proved uneventful, even boring by his standards. The laundry truck made its way out of the prison compound with an inmate driving, and a guard in the passenger seat. The process for delivering laundry to the outbuildings had been weak for some time. One guard accompanied the laundry truck, a miscalculation having its own repercussion. The fact this understaffing of security had gone on for so long determined the eventual outcome. It was an escaping prisoner's paradise.

The drop point at one of the outbuildings was of no special concern, until the inmate turned on the guard. The guard was killed. It didn't take much effort. Guards were often complacent after months of non-events. The laundry truck remained where parked, while the escapee trudged a bit through the woods to a waiting vehicle. No one suspected until hours later when the truck and guard did not return. It was then the hunt began.

Days Later

A visit was made to the nursing home in the early evening. A long overdue visit. It would tell him all he needed to know. Maybe. He had done his homework. He presented a fine appearance, well dressed and groomed. And polite. That was the key. A basket of flowers and a box of chocolate or two would seal the deal.

He approached the staff with overtures of grace. "I am hoping to visit Doris Lewis. I'm told she is a resident here," he offered as he approached the reception desk.

"Whom might you be?" was the reply from the overweight duty nurse.

"I am her younger brother, Robert Stephens."

She checked the records. "I'm sorry, sir. She has been a resident for two years, but we have no record of your authorization to visit."

"Oh! I'm sorry to know of this. I'm sure it's an oversight. I have been ill myself. I am just recovering from cancer surgery. It's been a hard road toward wellness with surgery, chemo treatments, and radiation. I'm in a good place now, and it all paid off. I was hoping to visit my sister. To let her know I'm okay. I'm sure she's been worried about me. By the way, this arrangement and this box of candy are for the nursing staff. The candy is the finest from Europe. You people deserve it. You all do such a fine job, from what I've been hearing."

He presented his driver's license when asked. Of course, it was forged. The female attendant looked at the license, and then at Mr. Stephens. My, but he was a handsome man, with a rugged, square jaw and penetrating blue eyes. Inwardly, she was swooning, and he knew it. Always a good judge of character, he calculated it was just a matter of minutes before he was permitted access to the main floor.

"Let me suggest this particular chocolate for you. It's my personal favorite," he offered while selecting one from the box. "It has a richly enticing nougat in the center," he said while taking her hand in his and placing the confection in her palm. He held her gaze while drawing a single finger seductively down the center of her hand before releasing his grip.

Her face took on a slow blush, averting her eyes from his. He knew he had her! She took a small bite of the chocolate.

"Oh my! That *is* delicious!" she declared.

"Then I will make it a point to bring some for you every time I visit."

"You are too kind."

"It's the least I can do for your excellent care of my sister. By the way, has she already had her dinner for the night?"

"Why, yes. Dinner was served over an hour ago."

"Then I can bring her dessert! She has a love for chocolate. When we were kids, we use to go to the corner store to buy our candy for the week after receiving our allowance. She always bought chocolate!" he shared, faking a giggle. "And she never shared!" He then took on a pouting look. "I would really hate to leave without seeing her this evening, if only briefly. Please, is there anything you can do?"

"Well," the nurse replied hesitatingly, "perhaps for a little while until we get the paperwork in order. I'll walk you to her room. Be mindful that she has good days and bad days. She doesn't always remember things or people."

"So I've heard. I'll keep that in mind."

They walked down a long hallway. Once outside the room, the nurse turned to the visitor. "This is Mrs. Lewis's room. I'll be at the front desk should you need anything, but please be brief."

"Yes, I will. And thank you," he said taking her hand in his. "I will be sure to find you before I leave," he said rather seductively.

A slow blush rose again across her round, pock-marked face before she walked away.

The visitor entered the room quietly. Doris Lewis sat in an overstuffed recliner watching a sitcom on the television. He noted the volume was rather loud. A hearing loss would make his visit more challenging, but not impossible. He stood awhile watching her. Dressed in a bright pink bathrobe and slippers, it appeared she was settled in for the night. Her hair was fully gray and thin, very thin, revealing patches of near baldness. Deep-seated lines marked her face and her lips were almost imperceptible. Doris Lewis was not aging well, he thought. She had lost all of her youthful beauty. Fully absorbed in the television show, she was oblivious to his presence until he spoke.

"You are looking well, Doris. It's good to see you again," he said softly, so as not to startle the old woman. There was no response. She couldn't hear him over the sound of the television. He would be forced to speak louder. Repeating himself so he could be heard, he waited.

Looking quizzically in his direction, she finally spoke. "Do I know you?" she asked, her voice tremoring.

"It's been a long time, Doris."

"Who are you?"

"I'm your brother, Robert. Don't you remember me?" he said, holding his breath. He was counting on her memory being poor today.

"No," she said quietly, all the time examining her visitor's face for recognition. "I'm afraid I don't know who you are at all."

"Don't feel bad. Your daughter told me you were living here and suggested I pay a visit to you. I'm sorry I haven't been here before now."

"My daughter?"

He could see she was struggling to remember. "Yes. Nichole Calavacchi." He remained quiet, hoping the name would spark a memory.

After a time her eyes took on a knowing.

"Nichole. Yes. That's my daughter, but she hasn't used that name in a long time."

"I didn't know that."

"No. Not for a long time."

"Perhaps that is why it was hard to get by the front desk. What do you call her, if not Nichole?"

"She's a doctor now. Did you know that?" the old woman asked.

"I think I did hear something about her becoming a doctor. You must be very proud. So her name is Doctor...

"DeShayne. Donna. That's what she's been called for some time now. You say she asked for you to come visit me?"

"Yes. The front desk people gave me her telephone number so I could get permission to visit you," he lied to the unsuspecting woman.

"Oh, that's nice. They are real good to me. Nichole... I mean, Donna, put me in a nice place. She comes to see me often."

"I'm so relieved to know this. I plan on seeing you more often myself, Doris. Would you like that?"

"I guess that would be all right. You say you're my brother?"

"That's right. Your brother, Robert. We had another brother, Richard, but he died a while back. Do you remember Richard?"

The woman was searching her brain for memory before finally answering. "No. I don't remember Richard."

"That's a pity. We three were very close when we were children. Oh, before I forget. I brought you some chocolates," he said, reaching over to transfer the small box to the old woman. "I remembered you love chocolates."

"Do I now?" was all she said as she took the box with a shaky hand.

"I was told not to stay long, Doris, but I will be back again. Would that be all right?"

"I suppose. What was your name again?"

"Robert," he said before quietly leaving the room.

He'd found out all he needed to know. Though he knew from the fat man his ex-wife's new name, he had to be sure. Supremely satisfied, he stopped at the front desk before leaving. The attending nurse was just ending a call on her cell phone. He waited patiently, flashing his best smile.

"You were right," he said convincingly, as she turned toward him at the counter. "She must be having one of her bad days. She didn't recognize me, or remember our deceased brother, Richard."

"Oh, I'm sorry. Perhaps another day then."

"Yes, for sure. Are you on duty this time every day?" he inquired, feigning an interest in the woman.

"I am. My days off are Sunday and Monday."

"Good! Then I will be sure to avoid Sundays and Mondays. That way I can look forward to having two charming people to visit."

Chapter Nine

Gavin Tandermann made an urgent call to Ken the moment he got the news.

Noting Gavin's phone number on his caller ID, Ken answered the call rather jubilantly. "Congratulations, Grandpa!" Ken said, fully expecting Gavin to gloat over the birth of the Larson twins.

"Thanks! But that's not why I'm calling. We've got a problem!" Gavin relayed with an urgent tone.

"Are Lacy Sue and the babies all right?"

"They're all fine. Listen. I just received word. Donald Calavacchi has escaped, and they have no idea where he is!" Gavin nearly shouted.

Ken was stunned. "What? When?"

"About a week ago. My contact was on vacation, and not notified until his return this morning. Where's Donna?"

"At her office. I'm heading over."

"I'll meet you there. Carole is on her way back from the café. She should be here any moment. We're both coming."

Ken was in a tailspin. This couldn't be happening. While they had talked about it on numerous occasions, the reality that Donna's former husband would escape from a maximum security prison and possibly endanger her life and that of her friends was beyond comprehension. Ken was taking no chances. He turned on his emergency lights and made a mad dash for her office. When he arrived, he was told she was in with a client. He instructed the receptionist, Kara Simms, to cancel all other clients for the afternoon and to lock all the doors. Understandably, the receptionist was alarmed.

"What's going on?" Karen asked, hands on her hips.

"Nothing that concerns you," Ken said rather abruptly.

The receptionist bristled at the response. "That doesn't float!" the feisty receptionist countered. She had known Ken for some time and liked him. This was the first he acted in a manner less than respectful. Something must be wrong. "Surely you don't expect me to just walk away for the day without concern. Also, I don't take orders from you. You don't pay me. So I will await the appropriate orders from my boss." She then sat down at her desk with her arms crossed defiantly.

Ken sighed. He had handled Kara all wrong. Of course, Donna's receptionist and friend would balk at his approach. She had dug in her heels and rightfully so. He had no choice but to bide his time, review the security system, and wait for the doctor to come out of the office with her patient. When Donna finally exited, she threw a curious look at Ken while she walked the client to the door. At that moment, Gavin and Carole entered the building. Donna could see Ken and her friends in frenzied conversation. Ever the professional, Donna continued a supportive exchange with her client before saying goodbye.

With her task complete, Donna immediately returned to the reception area.

"Okay, what have I missed? Are the Larson babies okay? Is Lacy Sue well?" Donna asked, assessing the matter given recent events.

Gavin and Carole remained quiet, their faces laced with concern. Ken came forward and placed his hands on Donna's shoulders.

"We need to go into your office," was all Ken said, mindful Kara was nearby, watching and listening.

Ken, Donna, and the Tandermanns entered Donna's office. Ken closed the door. No one sat.

Donna turned to Ken. "What gives?"

"We have received news. Your ex escaped about a week ago."

Donna's face drained of all color. She felt faint. Ken ushered her to the couch. Gavin poured a glass of water from the sideboard and handed it to her. "How could this have happened? Why, after all these years, and why are we just finding out about this now?" she asked. Her hands shook. Ken sat beside her, protectively taking her hand in his.

It was Gavin who spoke first. "My contact tells me a new inmate was recently transferred to the same maximum security prison your husband was in because of overcrowding at his former place. It was this new inmate who recognized your photo."

"My photo? Donnie had a photo of me posted in prison?" Donna asked in disbelief.

"Yes. In his cell. In exchange for protection, this prisoner told your ex what he knew about you."

"Who is this guy?" Ken asks angrily.

"Remember Chance Larson? The guy you arrested about ten years ago for drug smuggling? The guy who was using the church as a front for his drug operations?"

"My God!" Ken blurted. "Saul's father and Lacy Sue's father-in-law? What are the odds his fat ass connects with Calavacchi after all this time?"

"Slim to none, but it happened. Larson spotted the photo and told Calavacchi what he knew about you. Not only what he knew, but where he thinks you live. Calavacchi apparently had a friend on the outside who investigated and confirmed the claims, even the whereabouts of your mother. You have been watched and probably followed. Months after Chance gave him the information about you, Calavacchi broke out of prison, killing a guard in the process."

Carole had remained quiet until now. "So he knows she has changed her name, hair color, and she is a professional practicing locally?" she asked in a low tone, almost a whisper.

"We have to assume this to be the case," Ken replied. "We also have to assume Donna is his primary target, but he may use you or Gavin to get to her."

"Why now?" Carole asked, clearly unsettled.

It was Gavin who answered. "I don't think he had a clue how to find her all this time or else he would have made a move long before now."

"Donnie is a vengeful man," Donna said with more than a hint of resignation, her head bowed.

"I'll never forget at his sentencing when he turned to you and vowed to destroy you any way he could. That was the most chilling moment of the trial. So what's the plan? Carole asked, gathering strength, alternately looking at Ken and Gavin.

"We step up our protection!" Gavin said with an air of confidence he did not feel.

Donna looked up. "And do what? Our homes and businesses are wired for security with cameras up the wazoo. We have taken every self-defense course known to man. We are armed at all times and have concealed weapons permits. We have a call-in system to let each other know where we are at any given time. What more can we do?"

Ken spoke first. "You'll need to close your practice for a time until we catch him."

"Not on your life," Donna replied defiantly. "Surely you can't expect me to hide away until he is found?"

"It won't be forever," Ken said pleadingly.

Donna saw the fear in Ken's eyes. "Ken, you don't know that. Donnie is a highly resourceful individual. It could be some time before he makes his move, and then again, he may never come after us. I need to maintain some sense of normalcy in the meantime."

Carole spoke up. "I'm not taking any chances, not with two brand new grand babies in our lives." Carole looked directly at Gavin.

Gavin, being retired FBI, took the cue from his wife.

"We plan to wrap our property with underground electric security. It will allow us to know if someone or something enters the property without sounding an alarm, giving us the element of surprise."

Ken and Donna looked at each other before responding. "Whew! You two aren't playing are you?" Donna said.

"I don't see we have a choice. I suggest you consider it for yourselves," Gavin determined.

"What about the coffee shops, church, the mall, the bank, and the dozen other places we frequent? Are they all going to be wired?" Donna asked somewhat frantically. The enormity of the situation was getting to her.

No one spoke for a time. "Let's keep our heads," Ken said with an air of authority. "All three of you are armed at all times, am I right?" All three nodded. "And the guns are loaded?" Again, all three nodded. "An all-points bulletin has been issued. Calavacchi is not going to get far. We will just have to stay vigilant until he is recaptured. I have notified my team. They are on high alert."

Just then, there was a light knock on the door. It was Donna's receptionist. "Your two o'clock has arrived," she announced to her boss, scanning the room with intense curiosity.

Donna sighed. Fortunately, this particular client was in for a simple medications check. "I'll be out in a few minutes. Oh, and Kara, would you cancel my appointments for the rest of today and tomorrow and reschedule them? Something has come up requiring my attention," she ventured without explanation.

Kara nodded, although her face took on a questioning look before she closed the door. Something was definitely wrong.

Gavin gave Donna a nod of approval. "I'm going to make some phone calls and have the security people come out this afternoon. I'll be over to get Carole later on." Gavin's former position with the FBI was in security; all types of security.

"Send them over to our place when they're through with you, would you?" Ken requested.

"Already arranged!" said Gavin. "They'll be working into the night."

Ken pondered their next move. "Carole, would you be willing to drive Donna's car home? I'd like her to be with me when we enter the property."

"No problem," was the resolute reply from Donna's best friend.

Donna turned to Ken testily. "I may have a target on my back, but I can still drive!"

"You shall, but not today. I'll explain on the way. Carole, when you arrive at our home, do not get out of the car until I give you the okay," Ken admonished.

"Roger that!" Carole said with a nod. Carole knew Ken was in protective mode. "In the meantime, I'll stay with Donna until the added security is in place," Carole announced. "And, don't even think about protesting, girlfriend," she said feistily upon seeing the expression of disapproval forming on Donna's face. "Besides, Lacy Sue and the babies are coming home tomorrow afternoon. You and I can help settle them in. Gavin will get Mary from school early so she can welcome her baby brother and sister home."

"I have to admit," Donna returned, "that's a reunion I would love to witness."

As Donna got into the car after completing the short appointment, Gavin and Ken had a brief conversation out of earshot of the ladies. Ken then got behind the wheel, checked his rearview mirror to insure Carole was behind him in Donna's vehicle, and then proceeded toward home.

Ken glanced at Donna before speaking, reaching over to squeeze her hand. "You okay?"

"No. I'm numb. Shocked. How could I have not seen this day coming?"

"Don't be so hard on yourself. No one could have predicted this. The fact your ex has been so quiet for the last sixteen years has caused all of us to be less than vigilant, me included."

"Oh, Ken, if it weren't for you—" Donna couldn't finish, now completely overcome with emotion.

"Listen to me. Nothing is going to happen to you. I will not allow it! We're going to get this guy once and for all. I just need you to do as I say until we do, even though my requests may seem petty or extreme. Can you do that?" he asked gently.

Donna nodded. They drove the rest of the way in silence, both lost in their own thoughts.

It became clear how in the last ten years, cocooned in Ken's devotion, Donna had allowed herself to lessen her guard. If it wasn't for Gavin arranging for Don Calavacchi to be monitored all these years, they may not have found out about his escape.

How different her relationship with Ken compared to her marriage to Donald Calavacchi, a convicted drug lord. Donnie was lavishly generous with Donna. She wanted for nothing. Calavacchi had demands, however. First, she was forbidden to ask questions as to how he came to have so much money, despite the fact his business often took him away for long periods of time.

In addition, his wife had to be "dressed to the nines" when they welcomed Donnie's friends and business associates to their home. The guests were never-ending. Many of those people had given Donna the creeps. When she began to suspect her husband might be involved in illicit undertakings, she had created a plan to get into Donnie's office, the forbidden zone. Once she did, she downloaded files from his computer onto a memory stick. Once the authorities examined the files they arrested Donald Calavacchi, rounding up his business associates as well.

The authorities, knowing Donna was in danger, placed her in the Witness Protection Program, changing her name from Nicole Calavacchi to Donna DeShayne. With the help of Gavin and Carole Tandermann, her neighbors and friends, Donna reshaped her life, moving to Myrtle Beach, South Carolina, after obtaining her degree in psychiatry.

Her specialty in forensic psychiatry was how she met Ken Daniels ten years earlier. Ken, head of the Investigative Unit for Horry County, South Carolina, asked for her assistance in a gruesome murder investigation. He, having been divorced for some time, was taken with the curvaceous five-foot-three-inch beauty with thick, flowing auburn-colored hair, and a smile a mile wide. Divorced herself, harboring a past she was hiding from, Donna was hesitant to get involved with the detective of towering height and commanding presence. She noted, however, that in his presence she felt safe and secure. Highly respected professionally, Ken had a determination about his work she grew to respect. Never one to demand, he skillfully led his team toward many successfully resolved cases.

In little time, Ken and Donna fell madly in love. He was beside himself when he discovered she had a past she had not revealed. Nonetheless, after earnest conversation with both her and the Tandermanns, Ken understood her past, falling more in love with Donna than ever before. Shortly thereafter, she began living with him in his home on the river.

Upon arriving home, Donna noted Caleb Blackwell's vehicle. Donna went to open the passenger side door to exit, but Ken placed his hand gently on her shoulder. "I need you to stay here."

"Why is Caleb here?" she questioned.

"I asked him to meet me here. He and I will check the inside and outside of the house," he said determinedly. She acquiesced, having already promised to yield to Ken's process. She nodded and sat back in the seat. He left the vehicle, promptly locking it with the remote.

Ken then turned to Carole who had arrived in Donna's car, and held up his hand to signal she was to stay in the car as well. He then approached Detective Blackwell. Donna could see the two men converse before they turned toward the house. Moving slowly in its direction, they walked up the front steps and onto the porch. Ken was relieved to see the alarm was still lighted. Regardless, both detectives drew their guns and slowly entered the house.

It seemed forever before they exited, and when they did, they made a check of the property, as well as the garage and storage shed. Finally, before making their way back to the vehicles, they put their guns away. It was only then that Donna allowed herself to breathe again. Ken went to Carole first to let her know it was safe to exit the vehicle. He then used his remote to unlock the vehicle, opened the door, and took Donna's hand protectively in his while ushering her from the car.

"Wow! This is just like TV," Carole boomed, secretly unnerved.

Ken smiled slightly, glancing in Caleb's direction before turning to her. "Just so you know, we have two detectives with Gavin as we speak doing the same check on your home and property."

"I'll make the coffee!" was all Carole said, heading toward the house.

Despite the seriousness of the situation, Donna couldn't help but wink at Ken. They both knew Carole was not a woman of few words unless she was rattled.

Celebrating Lacy Sue and the babies' return from the hospital the next day served as a joyous distraction for Donna. Everyone gathered in the living room. Carole and Gavin were in high form, proudly hovering protectively over the entire family. Soon it was time for Gavin to get Mary from school. Once Mary entered the house she went immediately to her tiny brother and sister. Donna held little Gavin while sitting on the couch, and Saul rocked little Carole in a nearby chair.

"They sure are tiny!" Mary said in awe as she gazed upon them, going from one to the other and then back again. "Are they going to wake up?"

"They will when they're hungry," Saul answered. "Just like you used to do."

"Say, big sis," Donna ventured, "how about you hold your little brother for a while?"

"Sure. Will he wake up?"

"I don't think so."

Mary sat beside Donna on the couch, allowing the infant to be transferred to her lap. Donna showed Mary how to hold the baby, while Gavin took photos. It was an idyllic setting, a respite for Donna to forget the danger lurking about.

Chapter Ten

The spring season was yielding spectacular growth and color. It would only serve to enhance the Johnstown Flood Museum fundraising festivities.

The Tandermanns and Wests readily agreed to join the group for the weekend, delighted by the invitation several months earlier. Secretly, Ken was pleased the arrangements had been made and accepted by the other couples. Given the looming threat of Donald Calavacchi, Ken wanted the Tandermanns nearby. Not that he expected Calavacchi to make a move, but it was one less thing he had to think about while away.

Donna, Ken, the Callahans, the Wests, and the Tandermanns arrived at the Heiser House the day before the big event in the late afternoon. Exiting the vehicle, they viewed the grounds with awe. The spring season had outdone itself in a splendorous outflow of foliage and flowers. The presentation bore intent to regale. Surely, the hand of George Heiser was evident.

The place was abuzz with activity. Three large tents had already been set up to accommodate the reception, dining tent, and food preparation. Catering trucks were dropping off and caterers were setting up portable stoves, grills, and warming trays. Florists were delivering arrangements for each table.

The verandah, laced with a bounty of flowering vines in an inviting presentation, served as background for the small bistro-styled tables to be elegantly draped the next day, each with a vase of spring-colored flowers. The effect would prove to be charming.

George was busy directing the deliveries for the next day's grand event, when he spotted the group exiting their large rental van. After giving last minute instructions to a workman, he made his way over to them, with a broad, welcoming smile.

"You made it," he said to the group, shaking everyone's hand.

"We did! And we're so excited to be here," Donna exclaimed, looking around her. "George, the grounds are absolutely beautiful!"

"Thank you. While I would like to take credit, Mother Nature has been especially generous this year in her display of color, and, of course, my groundskeeper is a genius in his own right. He even plants a vegetable garden for me every year so I can serve fresh vegetables to my guests during the summer."

Just then, a small man approached George at a respectful distance and waited patiently to be noticed by the innkeeper.

"Oh, here he is now," George announced. "Bob Boykin, these folks will be guests of the inn this weekend. Gentlemen, ladies, this is the person responsible for the display of beauty you see before you, my groundskeeper, Bob Boykin."

The group offered greetings and complements to the man who gave an almost inaudible reply and seemed almost embarrassed by the attention. After conferring with George on a matter, the little man scurried off.

"He looks familiar," Donna said, trying to remember where she may have seen him before.

"Oh, you may have come across him at the Flood Museum. He does maintenance there on occasion. In truth, Bob is all over town doing this or that. He excels at whatever he does and, because he has no family in the immediate area, he is usually available for repairs, and whatnot. He is somewhat reclusive, but everyone adores him."

"Yes, now I remember," Donna returned watching the man walk away toward a riding lawn mower.

They were escorted into the house and assigned their rooms. George reminded them wine and cheese would be available in the "gathering room" before they left for dinner.

After they returned to the inn following dinner, George suggested they gather in another lovely glass-enclosed room in the back corner of the inn overlooking the rear yard. The garden room, as he referred to it, held a large variety of potted plants tastefully set about the room, complementing the comfortable leather couches, recliners, and exotic area carpets. Much to their surprise another unexpected delight greeted them as they looked out the window. To *ohs* and *ahs*, they feasted on a spectacular lighted display of twinkling lights draped in ceremonial fashion across the trees and ground growth. Timed to twinkle sequentially along the whole back of the yard, it would be visible tomorrow night from the guest tents as well. It was nothing less than breathtaking.

"Enchanting! I can see why this is the event of the year in Johnstown," Donna said, as George entered the room with after-dinner drinks for his guests.

"I wish I could claim credit for the idea, but once again Bob Boykin made the suggestion and installed the display. Even I could not have imagined its stunning affect. He's not finished yet, I'm told. He plans to come early tomorrow morning to install lighting along the front borders of the grounds along the circular driveway in time for the festivities."

The following morning they were presented with a beautiful breakfast buffet in the garden room, along with various coffees and juices. A beautiful flower arrangement adorned their table.

Shortly after breakfast, they drove to the National Johnstown Flood Memorial in South Fork. They took the ranger's advice from their previous visit and arranged for a ranger-led van tour of the path of the flood. Entering the modern building, they were greeted by a park ranger, paid their entrance fee, and toured the display of flood related photos and displays as well as a list of the dead. They had just enough time to watch a film outlining the destruction and related aftermath of the flood, before meeting the park ranger and boarding the van.

The ranger was a wealth of information. Donna was completely absorbed and impressed with his knowledge of the area and the time. They learned that in 1889, more than thirty thousand people lived in Johnstown, of which more than seven thousand men were employed by the Cambria Iron Works. Established nearly fifty years before the flood, the company was known for its technological innovations. Recognized as the largest producer of rails in the country, the mill found itself in desperate need of unskilled workers because of its recent success at mechanization.

A wave of immigrants from Europe settled in Johnstown and lined up to be hired by the mill, most never intending to stay in

America. One-third of these did return home. The future for the immigrants was difficult. Living conditions were poor. They were forced to live in towns less than inviting: Cambria City, Prospect, and Conemaugh, unsanitary immigrant towns struggling to survive. Worse yet, their jobs were dangerous. The better jobs with higher wages and safer working conditions were often given to native-born Americans. Efforts at organizing for worker rights were strongly discouraged, often resulting in unemployment. It was a hard life for the immigrants. Every member of the family had to work, even the women and children, to insure the economic survival of the family.

Donna and the group also learned of a lodge fourteen miles away from Johnstown, and of the man-made lake built ten years previous to the club's ownership. The lake, two and one-half miles long, and seventy feet deep, would comprise four hundred fifty acres at an elevation of four hundred feet above Johnstown. It was a rich man's playground, but not for long.

July 28, 1881, realized the club's grand opening. It was known as the South Fork Fishing and Hunting Club. Shortly thereafter, the decision was made to install screens at the spillways of the dam to prevent fish from being lost, an effort to reinforce the club as a fishing and hunting destination for the wealthy.

On May 28, 1889, the rains started over Kansas and never stopped, sweeping a path toward Pennsylvania. The winter proved to be especially wet in the region, soaking the mountain range soil to capacity.

The rains found their way to Pennsylvania and the Johnstown area by May 30, 1889, drenching the region further on top of the one hundred days of rain and snow that winter. Telegraph operators issued three warnings of a possible problem with the dam down the line clear to Johnstown.

The rains proved too much for the dam, neglected for years and eventually stripped of its discharge pipes. Adding insult to injury, the dam was patched and lowered in recent years to permit a two-lane road for the benefit of wealthy club members.

The group found the narrative by the park ranger chilling. They listened with rapt attention, asking questions along the way.

"Did *anyone* realize the dam was in peril?" Jeff West, Karly's father, asked.

"There was some attempt to contain the waters," the ranger replied. "It was noted that the spillway was clogged. Thirteen Italian immigrants were summoned to clear the debris in hopes of containing the water. It was too little, too late."

The driver continued on his way toward the communities impacted by the broken dam.

"This area is called Mineral Point. The town, comprising two hundred families, was just a mile from the dam. The town was completely destroyed when the dam broke at 2:55 PM on May 31, 1889. The flood waters carried away two hundred fifty-five houses. The residents had no warning. Sixteen residents of Mineral Point were killed."

"I guess I hadn't given thought to other communities impacted by the dam," Jim commented to the ranger.

"That's understandable, since the greater destruction happened in Johnstown. Before we finish our tour, however, you will be visiting Woodvale, a company town built by Cambria Iron Company."

"What's a company town?" Karly asked the ranger.

"Good question," the ranger replied. "It's a town in which all the housing, stores, churches, and schools are owned by the one company that is the only major employer in the area.

Woodvale was one such company town. Company towns were usually in remote locations where coal, metal mines, or lumber industries were the dominate employer. Woodvale housed one thousand people, many of them immigrant employees. It would realize a death toll of three hundred fourteen, and their town completely wiped off the map the day of the flood. In addition to Woodvale, other communities were impacted severely, such as East Conemaugh, Cambria City, and Millville. When it was all said and done, twenty of the sixty-six counties in the state had been flooded."

"I had no idea," Donna exclaimed.

The ranger continued on with the van tour, stopping periodically to allow the group to exit the van so he could share the event from various perspectives as the waters roared down toward Johnstown. In no time, they found themselves back at the National Johnstown Flood Memorial where they had begun their tour. The ranger shared another interesting observation before his guests exited the van at the end of the tour.

"In the end, it would be determined in the court of public opinion no respect was given for the natural resources of the region at the time. The land was stripped of timber and coal, and Johnstown itself was polluted with soot and smog. Keeping this all in prospective, the Johnstown Flood was the single most tragic event in the United States in the form of death toll up until the Twin Towers disaster of September 2011."

The group of eight thanked the ranger for an information-filled afternoon with handshakes and embraces of gratitude before heading back into the building.

"Where's the gift shop?" Carole asked with a hint of mission.

"I'm with you," Donna returned.

All of them ended up with books or mementos that would serve to remind them of their visit.

They arrived at the Heiser House with plenty of time to ready themselves for the evening's festivities. Upon exiting the vehicle, they stopped in their tracks. The grounds had been further transformed since their departure that morning. In the middle of the large circular driveway was an imposing lighted fountain surrounded by palm trees, potted flowers, topiaries, and plants of every description. It was a serene and welcoming sight. The group found themselves in a state of awe as they walked the inviting perimeter of the spectacular setting

"My goodness," Julie West exclaimed. "This is absolutely beautiful!"

Just then they heard a voice behind them. "We can thank Bob Boykin for this idea. Once again, he has outdone himself." George was standing with his hands in his pockets, looking immensely pleased by the accolades of the group. "Oh, by the way, I'll lay out some refreshments on the verandah before our other guests arrive. It's an awesome sight to see the carriages arrive with attendees dressed in their best."

They still had two hours before the start of the event. Everyone went back to their rooms to rest and ready.

Donna quietly came up behind Ken while he showered, placing her arms around his waist to draw him to her while laying her head against him. He turned slowly, kissing her

deeply. They had often made love in the shower. Ken marveled at how seductively she soaped his body, kissing and pleasuring him alluringly in spontaneous gestures of unabashed consecration. They muffled their moans of passion as their combined release gathered toward a crescendo. Afterward, they smiled and held each other while the waters ran over their bodies, both thinking of how lucky they were to have each other's love.

The carriages began to arrive. Ken and Donna, along with the rest of their group, gathered on the verandah, helping themselves to wine and refreshments as they sat or stood to watch the procession with rapt attention. As the driveway was too small to accommodate any additional vehicles other than those of guests staying at the bed and breakfast for the weekend, arriving guests were directed to park in a nearby field. They would then be assisted into magnificent horse-drawn carriages similar to those in use in the mid-1800s and delivered to the circular driveway of the Heiser House to be welcomed by the proprietor.

The first carriage to arrive held Thea Germaine, curator of the Johnstown Flood Museum, and the board of directors of the museum. The group looked stunning in their formal wear. George immediately stepped forward to assist Thea from the carriage, her eyes finding his with a smile before she stepped down.

"I'd say those two are an item," Carole remarked from her rocking chair on the verandah with a glass of wine in hand.

"You think?" Donna asked. "What makes you say that?"

"Body language, girlfriend. It's all about body language. Those two are speaking the same language, I can assure you."

Thea and the board of directors joined George, forming a reception line to greet their guests. The carriages continued their resplendent parade, delivering the governor and other dignitaries from across the state. The procession continued until the last of the guests arrived. All were escorted to the reception tent for wine, cocktails, and hors d'oeuvres after moving through the receiving line and having their photo taken by a nearby photographer.

Once inside the reception tent, guests would find photos lining the tent wall depicting various scenes from the 1889 Flood; a subtle reminder of the fundraising effort to take place that evening.

A table laden with pens and forms was available at the far end of the reception tent so guests could indicate and pre-order their dinner choices after a review of the extensive menu. George Heiser was insistent guests not be subjected to a buffet, but would be served their dinner while seated. After the group turned in their dinner choices, they meandered about with their drinks to look at the Johnstown Flood photos and timeline, periodically making a choice from an array of appetizers offered on trays by one of many smartly dressed waiters attending to the needs of the guests. A small orchestra played softly in the background, accompanied by the inviting sound of a harp. Two fully stocked bars were decorously placed, one on each end of the reception tent. The offerings were substantial and generously poured.

Jim and Karly found Donna and Ken looking at the photos. "I think I'm out of my league," Jim said in a whisper so as not to be overheard.

"Did you know the governor was going to be here?" Donna asked.

"George never said anything about who would be attending, but from the looks of things, I'd say he has connections all across the state," Jim returned.

"He is spending a fortune tonight. I understand he does this every year," Ken commented as he made a choice from a tray of appetizers presented by a roving waiter.

Just then Carole and Gavin, along with Jeff and Julie joined the group. They too took advantage of the offerings on the tray.

"There are enough jewelry and diamonds glittering in this tent to make a girl go blind," Carole said in her usual robust manner.

"I'll say," said Julie. "The governor's wife alone should be under a security watch with all the stones she's wearing."

"I've observed a high amount of security tonight," Jim returned

"So have I," Ken agreed.

"How can you tell?" Donna asked, looking about her.

"It comes with training," Gavin offered. "For instance, you have two guys who are within a three-foot radius of the governor and his wife at all times. One is scanning the crowd while the other watches as people approach him for conversation. They're not the only ones, however. Because of the number of dignitaries attending tonight, I'd say there is an inordinate amount of protection. While Carole was resting after our return this afternoon, I strolled out to sit on the porch. An hour before the event, a van pulled up toward the tents with three bomb-sniffing dogs. Twenty minutes later they were loaded back up and driven away."

"I don't get it," Donna ventured. "George Heiser is fronting this affair with his own money for the benefit of the Johnstown Flood Museum. What's in it for him?"

"He wouldn't be the first man to support something his lover was involved in," Carole said offhandedly.

Everyone looked puzzled. Donna offered an explanation. "Carole thinks George and Thea Germaine are lovers." No one made any comment. They all turned, however to see whether they could spot George and Thea in the crowd.

"This group is as subtle as a charging rhino," Carole blurted. "Go on, make it obvious we are talking about them. I need to give everyone a lesson in subtleties."

Gavin quickly changed the subject. "If I were a betting man, I would wager that George Heiser is a heavy political campaign contributor to garner the attendance of this many state representatives. I understand there are even several state Supreme Court judges in attendance. This affair may also afford a likely candidate an unspoken kick-off point for his or her campaign. I'm just guessing, mind you."

"In exchange for what?" Jeff asked.

"I tend to agree with Gavin," Jim inserted. "I'm certain there's political motivation behind tonight's affair. George could take all the money it's costing him tonight and make a direct contribution to the museum. Instead, he chooses to put on this gala event yearly. I've not lived in this state long enough to know the political terrain, but I'd say George is a mover and shaker kind of guy, and a highly effective one at that."

Just then, the announcement for dinner broadcasted over the loudspeaker. The guests moved to the dinner tent and took their assigned seats at beautifully laden tables of fresh flowers and candles. The inside perimeter of the tent was adorned with a variegated display of soft lighting, some twinkling, some changing color, others invitingly sequenced. The orchestra played soothing dinner music in the background. Bottles of the best wines were brought to the tables and heartily poured, while each lady was surprised with a single pink rose placed across her place setting by well-attired wait staff with impeccable skills.

The soups and salads were served before the main course, each guest receiving exactly what they had ordered earlier in the reception tent. Each course was presented with a lavish flair. The tent was abuzz with conversation and laughter.

"My salmon is to die for!" Carole exclaimed, fully enjoying her meal.

"This prime rib is the best I've ever eaten," Jeff chimed in. The accolades on the food continued as the group enjoyed their varied dinners.

Dinner plates were cleared before the arrival of desserts and coffee, with each gentleman receiving an expensive Cuban cigar at his place setting.

"George sure knows how to throw a party," Ken said, admiring his cigar.

Donna and Ken observed George and Thea visiting each table. They eventually came to their table.

"Are you enjoying yourselves?" George asked warmly as he scanned the group.

"Immensely," Jim replied for them. "I don't think I've ever enjoyed myself more. The food was delicious. We can't thank you enough."

"Yes, you have impeccable taste, George. Even down to pink roses for the women and Cuban cigars for the men," Donna added. George beamed at the compliments.

Thea Germaine looked at George proudly before adding to the conversation. "You may not know this, but the roses came from George's own greenhouse. He is an expert on roses, and chose a pink rose this year because the color represents grace, admiration, and gentleness."

"How romantic!" Karly swooned. The women were thrilled.

"The reception tent has been cleared," George commented. "We will be moving there in a few minutes to begin the auction. In the meantime, after-dinner drinks will be served. I have chosen several imported dessert wines I am especially fond of, but you will also have a choice of cordials, cognacs, and liquors as well."

"You are too good to us!" Julie West exclaimed. The group applauded in agreement. George bowed slightly before he and Thea moved on to the next table.

The guests eventually moved to the auction tent, many carrying after-dinner drinks. Chairs had been set up with an aisle down the middle.

"I've never been to a real auction," Donna whispered to Carole who sat beside her.

"Just don't scratch your nose. They'll take it for a bid." Just then, numbered paddles matching their dinner order numbers were handed to each guest. "Well…maybe you can scratch your nose after all." Donna laughed.

Thea Germaine preceded the auction with a glowing acknowledgment of George Heiser's support of the museum and the night's fundraising effort. The crowd stood to applaud George. He blew a kiss to his guests in return.

The auction, most of it artwork, yielded a surprising return, much better than in recent years, no doubt reflecting an improved economy. With the auction closed and extremely successful, George suggested a toast. Waiters rushed forward with trays of fluted glasses filled with expensive champagne. The toast was eloquently expressed by the host, and underscored with raised glasses. The sound of clinking glassware could be heard throughout the tent. Thea announced the dinner tent had been converted and now ready for dancing, ushering the group in its direction. Some of the guests lingered over the auctioned items that were successfully bid on to get a better look, while the new owners settled their accounts with the auctioneer before moving on to the entertainment area.

At one point a small crowd was especially dense around the framed piece involved in the bidding war, while other guests called for the waiters to refill their champagne glasses. It didn't take long before Donna felt somewhat dizzy with the start of a headache.

"Can we move to the entertainment tent?" she asked Ken. "It's too crowded right now. I think I need some air." Immediately, he walked her toward the sound of the orchestra. Once inside she began to feel better.

Smaller bistro-type tables had replaced the dinner tables and the orchestra played a variety of music through the evening. Most took to the dance floor, with George and Thea taking the lead. Ken and Donna danced a number of times before the announcement was made several hours later of the arrival of the carriages, signaling a conclusion to the evening.

Again, George and Thea, and the board of directors for the museum, formed a line to thank their patrons, wishing them a safe journey home. Guests were then escorted to a waiting carriage and assisted in boarding. One last gesture was made as each guest was assisted down from the carriage upon arrival at the field where their vehicles were parked. They were handed a small box of imported chocolates ornately packaged with a ribbon around it that read, *Thank you for the pleasure of your company*. Donna and Ken, Jim and Karly, Gavin and Carole, and

Jeff and Julie found a box for each of them on their beds upon returning to their rooms.

They were presented the following morning with another appealing breakfast offering in the garden room. Thea entered the room as they were eating.

"I trust you enjoyed yourselves last evening," she said, ever the lady.

Donna answered for the couples. "It will be an evening we will not soon forget."

"I'm pleased. Your generous donation was most unexpected," Thea said, turning to look at each person at the table.

Jim stood to shake Thea's hand. "It was the least we could do. You and George were so over-the-top in gracious hospitality."

"Please come visit again at any time. Do you have plans today?" Thea inquired.

"On our previous visit, George suggested we make it a point to visit Grandview Cemetery. We thought we might do that before heading home," Donna answered.

"Wonderful! You won't regret your decision." Thea shook hands with the rest of the group before leaving the room.

All went back to finishing their breakfast. Carole, never one to be outdone, offered an observation to no one in particular in her usual forthright style as she buttered her croissant. "I told you she and George are an item."

"Why do you say that?" Karly asked while stirring creamer into her coffee.

"Simple math. There are four guest bedrooms, and they have all been occupied by us. Where do you think she slept last night?"

Chapter Eleven

After saying goodbye to George, they arrived without incident at the Grandview Cemetery. Located above Johnstown in an area known as Yoder Hill, it appeared the group had the whole cemetery to themselves. They concluded most people would be at church this Sunday morning and the afternoon would probably see more visitors to the gravesites.

The Grandview Cemetery, George had informed them before they left, held the distinction of being the final resting place for many of the two thousand two hundred nine victims of the Johnstown Flood, but not all. Indeed, a large, granite monument dedicated to the "Unknown Dead Who Perished in the Flood at Johnstown, May 31, 1889" caught the immediate attention of the group upon arrival. They took numerous photos. The prominent twenty-one-foot-high structure, called the Monument of Tranquility, bore three life-size figures representing faith, hope, and charity. The thirty-five-ton granite tribute was established three years after the flood in a ceremony attended by ten thousand people, including the governor and numerous other prominent men from across the state.

Moving behind the monument, the visitors proceeded to a section called the "Unknown Plot" containing the bodies of seven hundred seventy-seven Johnstown Flood victims that could not be identified. A white marker for each of the unknown victims was set out in an imposing even pattern of impressive design.

Donna, reading from one of the books she'd purchased the day before after the ranger-led van ride, shared a paragraph with the others. "It says here this plot contains the remains of about seven hundred seventy-seven unknown victims of the flood, but because they wanted sixteen rows of fifty-one stones per row, they ended up with eight hundred sixteen markers to give the plot more symmetry."

"Well, it's a striking, but sober reminder" Carole offered, "symmetry or no symmetry."

Donna continued to read aloud so the others could hear additional tidbits of information. "During the centennial anniversary of the flood in 1989, more than seven hundred thousand people visited the Johnstown Flood Memorial and the Unknown Plot here at Grandview Cemetery."

They wandered the grounds looking at other grave sites, determining by the date of death which ones were known flood victims. In time, they came upon the monument to Daniel Morrell and the Morrell family plot.

"I'm trying to remember what the van driver told us about this guy yesterday," Ken said to no one in particular.

"Wasn't he the manager of the Cambria Iron Works who tried to warn the club members the dam needed upgrades, even supplying the club with the engineer's report?" Julie West asked.

"Yes, and his concern was ignored. The monument shows he died four years before the flood," Jim answered.

They continued to wander about talking among themselves, mindful of the time if the six of them were to catch their flight early that evening. On their walk back to the rental van, Donna noted movement near the cemetery office. She turned to look and was surprised to see Bob Boykin.

"Isn't that Bob Boykin?" she asked Ken for confirmation.

"Sure is. I wonder what he's doing here."

"I didn't see him at all during the festivities last night, but I want to tell him what a wonderful job he did on the grounds and lighting." Donna began to walk toward the mousey, elfin-like man, but when she set off in his direction he was gone. Puzzled by the disappearance, she made her way where he had been standing and looked about but found no one.

"That's strange. He was here a minute ago."

"Who was here a minute ago?" Carole said, coming up on her friend.

"Bob Boykin. You know, the groundskeeper for George Heiser."

"Oh, you mean Yoda." Donna and Ken laughed. "Well, doesn't he look like Yoda from *Star Wars*?"

"I hadn't gone there in my head, but now that you mention it," Donna said, still giggling.

"I'm headed to the ladies room," Carole announced, and took off in the direction of the outdoor facilities.

Donna shook her head, never failing to be amused by Carole's observations on life and people.

"I would think he would be back at the bed and breakfast overseeing the dismantling," Ken commented.

"He appears to be shy and withdrawn, but to purposely walk away when he saw us is a bit rude."

"Maybe he didn't see you. Let's head for the van. I'd like to get an early start."

This kill had been especially easy. The opportunity hadn't been seen until the last minute. A different approach was planned until unexpectedly faced with an alternative that would prove to be just as effective, but safer. Chuckling afterward, a self-satisfied smile would be worn for several more days. The gods were especially good this time! Two goals had been accomplished. There was no stopping now!

The usual shower and disposal routine was repeated when returning home. Once again a return to the cupboard to retrieve the fifty-year-old bottle of Scotch was in order, a silent salute for an especially successful outcome. An added measure of the glorious liquid was poured. It was well-deserved. The news would get out in several days. There was no time to gloat. The next kill had to be researched and planned.

Donna and Ken left Carole and Gavin after brunch at their favorite breakfast restaurant the Sunday after their return from Pittsburgh and headed for the assisted-living center to visit Donna's mother. Donna never knew what to expect on these occasions since her mother often did not recognize them if she was having a bad memory day. On occasion, however, her mother would greet them warmly, clearly acknowledging them both by name.

Walking down the hall toward her mother's suite, they were greeted by the attending nurse as they passed the front desk.

"Good afternoon, Dr. DeShayne, Mr. Daniels," the nurse acknowledged. "Doris is having an in-and-out day so far."

That usually meant there were moments of recognition, but then they would fade, sometimes in mid-sentence. To Donna that was better than no recognition at all.

"Thanks, Heather," Donna replied warmly as they headed in the direction of her mother's room.

"Oh by the way, your uncle is a charmer. He was here three times last week."

Donna stopped and looked at Ken. Retracing their steps, they returned to the desk.

"Uncle?" Ken asked.

"Why, yes. Mr. Stephens."

Their faces took on a look of concern. "Heather, to my knowledge, my mother does not have any siblings. Are you sure this Mr. Stephens has the right Doris?"

"Oh my. That's disconcerting. He brought in a photo of their deceased brother and told stories of them as children," the nurse replied.

Ken stiffened, and Donna's face took on a look of alarm.

"Is something wrong?" the nurse inquired.

"Not necessarily," was all Ken said before taking Donna by the arm to continue toward her mother's room.

Entering quietly, they found Doris Lewis watching a western on TV.

"Hi, Mom," was all Donna said.

"Hello, Doris. How are you doing today?" Ken asked the aging woman.

Doris looked up in their direction. "Are you my daughter?" she asked, confusion registered on her face.

"Yes, I am." Donna knelt at her mother's lap to take her hands in hers. She watched her mother's face scanning hers. Shortly there was an unexpected sign of recognition. "Oh, yes. You're Nichole."

Donna whipped around to look at Ken. Her mother hadn't called her by that name in years.

"No, Mom. My name is Donna. Remember? I changed my name to Donna."

"Your uncle still calls you Nichole," Doris replied.

"Mom, I don't have an uncle."

"Then who is that man?" Doris asked, pointing an unsteady finger toward a photo on her nightstand.

Ken reached over to pick up the framed photo, handing it to Donna.

Taking it, she peered at the picture and began to shake. Ken was beside her in an instant. "What is it, Donna?"

"It's him," she said in a labored whisper, fear registered on her face. "It's Donnie."

Staring back at Donna was a recent photo of her mother with Donald Calavacchi. He was all smiles.

Ken alerted local law enforcement and sent out another APB to alert authorities the escaped convict had been sighted in the area. Ken then sent a text to Gavin, who showed up with Carole immediately at the nursing home. Caleb Blackwell and several other officers arrived before the Tandermanns. Blackwell was already busy questioning the nurse, Heather Blaine.

Ken suggested Donna take her mother for a walk in her wheelchair around the facility, explaining he needed to dust Doris's room for fingerprints. The Tandermanns found Donna and Doris at a table in the lounge drinking hot chocolate. Gavin noticed Donna's hands shaking.

"Did you know I had a brother younger than me that died?" Doris questioned. "Now why did I not know that?"

Gavin and Carole sat at the table protectively, one on each side of Donna. Ken soon entered the lounge. He had overheard Doris's questions.

"Doris, did Mr. Stephens ask you about Donna?" Ken ventured when he took a seat at the table.

She sat there for a bit, searching her embattled mind, trying to remember. Then her eyes lit up. "Now I remember. He asked about Nichole. I told him you were a doctor now," she said proudly. "He brought me chocolates. They were delicious."

"Do you remember if he asked where Donna, I mean Nichole, lived?" Ken asked gingerly.

"No...I don't remember. Now, I wonder what I did with those chocolates." It was clear Doris Lewis was not going to be of further help.

Just then, a uniformed officer appeared in the doorway of the lounge. Ken rose and approached the man. They had a brief conversation before Ken returned to the table. Apparently the fingerprinting of Doris Lewis's room was complete.

"Donna, perhaps your mother would like to go back to her room to rest," Ken suggested.

"I am a little tired. I usually take a nap in the late morning before lunch," Doris offered.

Donna settled her mother in and kissed her on the forehead before leaving. "Do I know you?" her mother asked. Clearly, Doris had once again escaped to the recesses of her mind.

The Tandermanns walked Donna to the lobby where Ken waited with Caleb Blackwell.

"Find out anything?" Gavin inquired, ever the ex-FBI agent.

"The fingerprints match those of Donald Calavacchi," Ken announced.

"The guy has a lot of balls coming to the nursing home and having a picture taken with Donna's mother," Carole fumed.

"He wants Donna to know he can find her at any time," was all Gavin said. Carole elbowed Gavin hard. He winced. "Sorry, Donna. Sometimes I veer off the track in the sensitivity department."

Donna returned a weak smile. "What now?" she asked wearily.

"We step up security," was all Ken said.

"Is my mother in danger?"

"I don't think so, but we're not going to take any chances. We're posting security at the doors, at least for a while. We might have to look into moving her to another facility, although I don't think he wants to harm your mother. He wanted to get your attention," Ken explained.

"Well, he certainly succeeded in that!" Carole boomed. "And his point is…?"

"It's like Gavin said. He wants me to know he's around and watching," Donna answered dejectedly. "Donnie was always the control freak. Why would I think he would ever change?"

"Gavin, would you take Donna home? I have some loose ends to tie up back at the office," Ken explained.

"I'll take her to our place. You can pick her up afterward."

A week later, Donna and Ken attended the church baptism of the Larson twins. Jim and Karly, Karly's parents, Jeff and Julie West, and Caleb and Sienna Blackwell and their sons attended the ceremony as well.

Carole and Gavin, as godparents, stood on either side of the parents, Lacy Sue and Saul. Mary stood proudly, holding her baby sister, Carole, while Saul held baby Gavin. Both infants were asleep. Afterward, a luncheon was held in a private dining room at a local restaurant. Nearly everyone took turns holding the babies, with Mary hovering protectively.

After lunch, Karly's parents left for home and the Blackwells took their leave to visit their children's grandparents. The Larson family thanked everyone and eventually left as well. Donna and Ken, the Callahans, and the Tandermanns lingered a bit more over a second cup of coffee.

"Great food, but lousy coffee," Carole announced, ever the coffee bean expert. "I'll have to have a private talk with the owner. Say, Megan should be as big as a house by now."

"We're waiting for word any day that we are grandparents!" Donna said enthusiastically. "I want to have as much fun as you and Gavin seem to be having."

Shortly thereafter, everyone made their way to the parking lot. Donna was the first to head to the car after hugging the others who were still in conversation. It was then they heard her scream. Rushing to her side, they found her shaking uncontrollably, her face distorted with distress. They looked in the direction of where she finally pointed.

On the hood of the car was a single black rose.

Chapter Twelve

Jim had just returned to the office after their long weekend in South Carolina visiting with family and friends. He was still rattled Donald Calavacchi had been outside the restaurant while they were having lunch, and its effect on Donna. It was discussed, and then decided Donna should be provided with private security until the escaped convict was apprehended. Even still, Jim felt helpless being so far away.

That afternoon, however, another occurrence came to Jim's attention. He read the report a second time before he placed the call.

He was surprised Donna picked up on the third ring. "I'm checking in for two reasons," Jim said slowly. By nature, Jim had a slow manner of speech. "One is to find out how you're doing this afternoon."

"I'm okay for now. I have security standing outside my office all day. He showed up this morning at the house and drove me to work. My receptionist, Kara, is a little freaked out. I had to conjure up an excuse as to why he was there. I don't think she's convinced. What's the second reason?"

"Huh?"

"You said you were checking in for two reasons. What's the second reason?"

There was a moment of quiet before Jim spoke. "There's another body."

Donna was stunned. "The Croaker?"

"It looks that way."

"Then there was a pin on the victim," she said for confirmation.

"Yes, and it's an exact match to the others."

She hadn't realized she was holding her breath until she let out a long sigh. "Who's the victim?"

"Now that's the thing. It's too close to home if you ask me," Jim replied.

"What do you mean?"

"The deceased was a guest at the Johnstown fundraiser. A state Supreme Court judge no less. He died in his office Monday morning."

"What? There must be some mistake!"

"I'm afraid not. I have the report right in front of me. It's hitting the news outlets as we speak. I'll email it to you."

"Then everyone will know we have a serial killer?" Donna asked cautiously.

"Not necessarily. We left mention of the pin out of our report to the press for a number of reasons. We don't want this turning into a media circus."

"I'm relieved," she returned. "Who is the judge?"

"Judge Barrett Reeder. I'm told Judge Reeder was on the bench for seventeen years. They found him at his desk yesterday afternoon. We have not publicly challenged the initial claim by newspapers he died of natural causes, however, we have discreetly petitioned the family to agree to an autopsy."

"Because of the pin and its possible connection to the other poisonings, I would think."

"Exactly. We should know something in a day or so. I'll call you with the findings when they come in."

Donna sat back in her chair, digesting this new information after ending the call. Between her own precarious situation and those related to the Croaker case, her head was spinning. If truth be known, however, she was somewhat grateful for the distraction the Croaker provided from her own worries. Just then, Ken called.

"Hey, beautiful, whatcha' up to?" he asked.

"I'm taking a break. I just got off the phone with Jim." Donna filled Ken in on the latest killing.

"A sitting judge, eh? Wow. Our killer is getting in pretty thick. How's security treating you?"

"I guess okay. Just his size alone is intimidating. Kara is asking a lot of questions."

"It's just temporary," Ken replied.

"I hope. The thing is, this reminds me of my life with Donnie. He always had one of his goons watching me. It's like I've gone back in time."

Ken didn't say anything at first. "Do you remember that road construction sign we saw on the highway a few years back, the one that said 'A temporary inconvenience for a permanent improvement'? That's the way you have to look at this situation, Donna. It's temporary, and when it's all over, you won't ever have to look over your shoulder again. I promise."

How she loved this man! "What did I ever do to deserve you?"

Jim called Donna again several days later with an enlarged report on the killing of Judge Reeder. "The judge was poisoned, as we suspected," he said without preamble.

"How was it administered?"

"Do you remember the small box of imported chocolates waiting for us in our rooms the night of the fundraiser?"

"Yes I do. They were awesome."

"What we didn't know at the time is that each guest at the dinner also received one at the end of the night when they were returned to their vehicles. In Judge Reeder's case, however, all six chocolates were cleverly injected through the box with massive amounts of tetrodotoxin. Unfortunately, the judge loved chocolate. He was dead before he ate the fifth piece."

"Pufferfish poisoning. It's tasteless, quick and lethal."

"It is almost the perfect poison," Jim added.

"He must have taken them to work with him Monday morning," Donna said, thinking out loud.

"Chocolates for breakfast."

"So there was someone at the party who had it out for the judge and wanted him dead," Donna ventured. "Do we have the guest list?"

"We've already requested the list from George Heiser."

"You say the frog pin was on the clothing of the judge?"

"On his robe no less. He was scheduled to enter court, but when he didn't show up, they went looking for him. He was already dead when they found him."

"Jim, if this was the doings of our serial killer, then he is getting sloppy. He had to be at the affair to inject the box, don't you think?"

"I agree. Russ Carotti, who I just got off the phone with, thinks our killer may be getting overly confident. Russ says he took quite a chance killing a well-known judge. He had to know the authorities would be all over this."

Donna didn't respond, but let Jim continue. "There's something else of interest. Remember the auction and the bidding that night? Remember the sparing between the two gentlemen for that particular art piece?"

"I do. The bidding war seemed to go on and on. It was getting tense. The crowd loved it though, if I remember."

"It was the judge who won the bid!"

"Oh? Who was the other bidder?"

"I'm told it was Keith Demoine, a local banker."

"Any bad blood between the two of them?"

"We're checking. Demoine has a brother who is an attorney as well, specializing in bankruptcy law. Another thing," Jim continued. "It appears the art piece Reeder won at the auction is missing."

"Missing? How can that be?"

"It hasn't been located as of yet, so we are now assuming it was stolen. Now here's the interesting part."

"You mean this hasn't been interesting so far? I am completely flabbergasted. I can't imagine what else you have that can top this."

"The art piece is very valuable and belongs to George Heiser."

"What do you mean it belongs to George Heiser? If the judge won the bid, how can it belong to Heiser?"

"Everyone who wins the bids recognize the art they won is on loan for one year only. They have to sign papers acknowledging George Heiser as the rightful owner and the loan arrangement is temporary. Each piece is heavily insured, but until now there has never been an incident of theft or damage."

"So the auction is a pseudo-auction," Donna surmised aloud.

"Precisely. For fundraising purposes only."

"So that's why the beginning bids were so low to begin with. I understand now. It was a puzzle to me at the time. Do you think the killer stole the painting as well?"

"We haven't determined such a thing yet. Apparently, it was to have arrived at Judge Reeder's office within several days of the auction. It hasn't shown up, and there is no shipping manifest to be found."

"So the judge was killed before the anticipated arrival of the artwork. I'd say the firm responsible for shipping the piece needs to be questioned."

"We are questioning everyone connected to the festival. The suppliers, the bartenders, waiters, grounds people, florists, and the guests."

"Do we know anything else about the fellow who bid against Reeder?"

"We have it on good authority he left the party pretty wasted. It was arranged for an attendant to take him and his wife home before it became too obvious to others. George had their vehicle discreetly delivered to their home early the next morning."

"George seems to cover all the bases, doesn't he?" Donna asked.

"In this case, the gentleman, being a respected banker in town, required some discreet handling. I'm guessing George does a lot of business with the bank. He may have been acting to save the fellow from embarrassment."

"Let's hope that's all it is. You've got a substantial number of people to question."

"More than three hundred," Jim confirmed. "We've called in reinforcements."

"Good luck."

Donna spent the entire weekend curled up on the couch poring over the books she had purchased while visiting the Johnstown Flood Museum and the Johnstown Flood Memorial. She not only found the events fascinating, but also could not ignore a gnawing feeling the killings were somehow related to the Johnstown event of 1889, despite the absence of evidence. In her mind, there could be no other explanation for the odd depiction of a frog with a fishing rod on the gold lapel pin. To have another pin show up shortly after a fundraising effort on behalf of the museum seemed especially significant. The question remained, however, how did the pin find its way onto Reeder's robe?

She shared her thoughts with Ken when he came in at the end of the day after spending the weekend painting their outside storage shed.

"I think it's a stretch, Donna," he said, listening to her while shaving. "All those people are dead now. The only things left are those items and photos in the museum and the memorial. George Heiser is a third generation flood survivor, and yet, even he, with all of his wealth and influence, has never seen a pin like that associated with the flood. Still," he continued after toweling off his face, "you've proven me wrong before, my little wizard."

He kissed her endearingly. He then kissed her again, longer and deeper this time.

"How about you let this little wizard perform some magic?" she said breathlessly, leading him to the bedroom.

"I'm a sucker for a good magic show."

Chapter Thirteen

George Heiser was livid. He had been getting phone calls and text messages all day from friends and acquaintances who attended the Johnstown Museum fundraising event the previous weekend. The questioning by the authorities into the death of Judge Reeder had begun and the town was abuzz with rumor and speculation. They were calling George for an explanation, for which he had none. Still, such a major operation by authorities had him curious. What was really going on? How would these events affect next year's donations? He had to have answers.

Jim let the phone call go to voicemail. He had nearly two dozen people to question today, and he was not about to let himself be distracted by anyone, including George Heiser. He would call George later, not wishing to alienate the man who had been so gracious to them just two weekends ago.

Jim, with authority from the Federal Bureau of Investigation, organized teams of interrogators with specifically-crafted questions in an effort to swiftly identify inconsistences and personal timetables. This effort would continue for nearly three days. The responses would be correlated electronically at the end of each day, adding the next day's responses to the data, and the day after that until they had a computer generated overview from nearly three hundred fifty people. The teams would then be assigned to those who were chosen by the computer for another interview process for any number of reasons, this time allowing the teams to ask their own questions after review of the data.

It would be late evening before Jim found the time to return Heiser's phone call. George noted the incoming call on his cell phone and knew who it was before he answered.

"Mr. Heiser, I apologize for the late hour. Is this a good time, sir?"

"Jim, thank you for getting back to me. Yes, it is a good time. I'm just sitting here having a vintage glass of wine after a hectic day. I understand your day has been busy as well."

"Yes sir, it has," was all Jim offered by way of explanation.

When Jim did not comment further, Heiser pressed on. "I was saddened to learn of the death of Judge Reeder, Detective. He was an ardent supporter of the museum and well-respected all across the board in this state. It seems to me, however, there is considerable effort being expended by the authorities in their investigation. The newspapers indicated he died of natural causes. I understand, however, guests from the fundraiser are being interviewed. It seems to be a little over the top if the judge's death was a simple heart attack. Wouldn't you agree?"

Jim knew he had to respond prudently. "I understand your concern, Mr. Heiser, however there is a small irregularity we are investigating, nothing more."

Heiser was slow to respond. "Your visit here in the winter was an investigative one as well. Can you tell me if that investigation is related to the current events surrounding the death of Judge Reeder? I ask because I learned today my painting is missing, the one Judge Reeder successfully bid on. Is that the irregularity?"

Jim thought quickly. Heiser knew they had toured the South Fork Hunting and Fishing Club off season by special request through the National Park Service. Heiser's special connection to Thea Germaine could have served as a conduit for that kind of information despite her assurance at the time she would keep their conversation protected. Heiser's question, however, gave him a quick way out.

"You are very perceptive, Mr. Heiser. We found it odd the shipping manifest and painting are both missing. It could simply be a clerical issue you understand, but we need to rule out any foul play."

"So you think the painting is related to Judge Reeder's death," Heiser said, more as a statement than a question.

"Our official position is the judge died of natural causes, nothing more. Still, let me ask you something," Jim interjected. "Was there anyone who had a grudge against the judge and wanted to make him look bad by taking the painting?"

"The judge had a long history on the bench. I'm sure he was forced to make decisions less than popular. I knew of no one who harbored any resentment toward him, however."

"One more question. Did anything unusual happen in the days prior to the fundraiser?"

"Like what?"

"Anything out of the ordinary."

"It gets pretty hectic here the week before the event. There are a million details. Fortunately, I have Thea and Bob to assist, but no, nothing unusual happened, other than the delivery to Ms. Germaine of another envelope again this year."

"Envelope?" Jim questioned.

"It's nothing really. It arrives like clockwork every year and is exactly the same thing as the year before, and the year before that. We have come to ignore it."

"How long has the arrival of this envelope been going on?" Jim asked, highly intrigued by the turn in the conversation.

"Oh, about twenty years. It's not at all threatening, just a listing of the dead from the Flood of 1889. In the early years, we attempted to track its source, but failed."

"Does Ms. Germaine keep these envelopes?"

"Now, that I can't say. You'll have to ask her. Is this important?"

"I think it's another small irregularity that needs to be looked into, is all," Jim judiciously replied.

Jim exited his car with two lab technicians two days later only to find George Heiser outside the Johnstown Flood Museum waiting for them. This was a surprise to Jim.

"I didn't expect to find you here, Mr. Heiser," Jim said, shaking his hand.

"I hope I'm not intruding. Ms. Germaine asked me to come. She thought I might be able to offer assistance," he returned.

Jim found it odd Thea Germaine made this request. When he inquired of her as to the various envelopes, she assured him she had indeed kept each one, but had no idea of the source. It seemed to Jim that Heiser was hovering, and more than a little protective.

The curator led Jim and the two lab technicians, along with Heiser, to a conference room across the hall from her office.

There they found, spread out in date order, twenty envelopes, each containing a list of those killed in the flood of 1889, all identically written on the same stationary. Upon examination, there were no postmarks or stamps on the envelopes.

"These were obviously hand-delivered," Jim said to no one in particular. He nodded to the two technicians who immediately went to work.

"What do you hope to find?" Thea inquired, watching the men take out their supplies.

"Fingerprints, for one," Jim answered. "And perhaps a hint of the envelope's origin."

"Oh, dear. I'm afraid you'll find my fingerprints. Even George's and the board of directors. I have surmised these are the acts of someone highly compulsive. I admit I was concerned for the first three years, but when nothing of significance happened, I began to ignore them and simply filed them away. I've come to expect them each year, really."

"How were they delivered?"

"They were slipped under my office door. You may even find my shoe prints on the first several envelopes. I've grown so used to these I just expect one to appear on the 30th of May each year when I unlock my office. I have even come to look for them, really. "

"Why would someone create a list?" Jim asked.

"Especially since it is information we already have," Germaine added.

"It strikes me our mystery person is someone who has access to the building. How else could these have been slipped under your door? I may ask to go through your personnel records, Ms. Germaine."

"Yes, of course, if it is absolutely necessary. Quite honestly, I just don't see it as being prudent. No crime has been committed. It's a simple listing of the dead. Does this have something to do with Judge Reeder's passing?" she asked.

"No, not really. This matter came up in a previous conversation with Mr. Heiser, and I decided it should be looked into," was all Jim offered by way of explanation. It sounded weak, even to him.

The lab men asked permission to take Germaine's and Heiser's fingerprints, which they immediately granted. Jim then asked permission to take the envelopes and their contents back with him to study, with assurances they would be returned to the museum as soon as possible. Again, his request was granted. Upon finishing up, the lab men gathered their things.

"Ms. Germaine, I want to thank you for your cooperation," Jim said, extending his hand.

"If you discover something significant, would you be kind enough to call me? This has been a puzzle for quite some time. I would be relieved to discover who the sender is after all these years."

"I promise I will call with any development."

George Heiser walked Jim and the technicians to their vehicle, while Thea remained behind to take a phone call.

"The next time you're in the area, Detective, please give me a call."

"I will, Mr. Heiser."

"Please, call me George. All my friends do," the man replied amicably.

Jim had the distinct impression George Heiser was uncomfortable with their visit.

The investigation into the death of Judge Barrett Reeder yielded several interesting developments, one of which was the threat made against the judge by an offender he had sentenced to a long prison term years earlier for fraud and embezzlement. The guilty person had served his time and had been released months before. Further investigation, however, found the ex-convict was overseas at the time of the murder.

There were then the two ex-wives of the judge who had nothing good to say about the judge. It seems Reeder had used his authority to sway the divorce court in ordering a less than favorable financial settlement for both wives. The second wife was especially vicious in her verbal assaults whenever mention of her ex-husband came up. The third wife had signed a prenuptial. The judge was taking no chances the third time around.

Jim continued to keep Donna apprised of news coming from the investigation.

"Did you get a copy of the envelopes I sent?" Jim asked on an early morning phone call, referring to the envelopes given to him by Thea Germaine.

"I did. I glanced at them briefly, but I honestly don't see how the envelopes and the list of the dead from the flood connect with the Croaker."

"It probably doesn't," Jim admitted.

"I will say, what remains more puzzling is how the frog pin was attached to Judge Reeder's robe. To think the Croaker had such close access to the judge is a scary thought."

"We're puzzled as well. We're questioning his family and law clerks."

"The stolen art is another question. This is certainly a departure for our murderer. Do we know anything about the art piece?"

"This country boy got a lesson in art yesterday. It seems the piece is an original by the world-renown Belarusian artist Leonid Afremov. He currently lives in Israel. His work can be reviewed and purchased on his website. He's most noted for his use of knives and oil in his paintings, which apparently distinguishes him from other artists, leaving his works immeasurably different and unmistakable. He's gained impressive recognition for the vivid use of bright colors. I'm told his work is highly sought after by those wanting an Afremov original. The artist is aging. Upon his death, the value of his work will skyrocket."

"So we know the painting stolen was valuable and not a knock-off," Donna said more than asked.

"George Heiser was able to produce the purchase order, original invoice and proof it was heavily insured. I'd say its valuable, and will just grow in value over time."

"Yes, I imagine it will, but George had it insured, so he won't be too impacted. How are the interrogations going?"

"We're getting there, but no definitive leads yet. We have a huge hole in tracking down the names of the horsemen, waiters, bartenders, and kitchen staff on duty the day of the fundraising event. The catering people did not do due diligence in getting the names of all those working that night. They were paid in cash at the end of the evening. That fact didn't make my day."

"So there's a cold trail, at least on that end," Donna concluded.

"Precisely. Not to mention the owner may be facing a tax avoidance issue if the state gets wind of it."

"I plan on taking the weekend to study the facts we have so far on the Croaker. As my friend Carole would say, 'When I strike oil, I'll let you know.'"

Jim smiled. "How are she and Gavin making out as grandparents to the twins?"

"They are in heaven! Those babies and Mary are surrounded by two fussing and clucking grandparents. There's not a thing they would not do for them or their parents. They are definitely pulling out all the stops."

"I figured as much. How are you handling this thing with your ex, if I may ask?"

"One day at a time, Jim. One day at a time. Will we see you and Karly's parents for our July 4th barbecue?"

"You bet. Karly and I have already put in for time off for an extended weekend. My in-laws will have just gotten home the week before from their trip to Holland. Be prepared to look at lots of photos."

"By some miracle, I would love to see the Croaker case solved by then. It would be a year and another murder committed since you invited me in to examine the matter."

"It's a stubborn one, for sure. Our killer is very clever. Whomever it is will slip up sooner or later, and when that happens, we'll be there!"

Today the Larson family celebrated Mary's eleventh birthday. The festivities included pony rides at a nearby farm and a hayride to a secluded tree-filled grove on the farm where Gavin and Carole would feed twelve little girls hot dogs, chips, drinks, birthday cake, and ice cream. They were encouraged to dress as cowgirls. Mary, ever the tomboy, sported a cowboy hat, western boots, chaps, and a double holster with toy guns. The grownups, Donna and Ken included, were having the time of their lives overseeing the girls in various team sports, foot races, and apple bobbing.

No one had any idea they were being watched and photos taken with a high-powered distance camera. He recognized the Tandermanns from years ago, but the other young couple, with the babies and the little girl, was new to him. No matter. His interest was in his former wife, and her boyfriend. Soon he would have their daily pattern down pat. Despite the added security when the boyfriend was not around, he would discover the weakness in their schedule. It was only a matter of time. He had all the time in the world.

Chapter Fourteen

Donna walked on her treadmill the following morning. Ken had strongly discouraged visits to the gym until her fugitive ex-husband was apprehended. He reasoned it was one less place his team had to be concerned with. The immediate gift of a treadmill and home gym made the decision more palatable, at least for the short term. Always a physical fitness junkie, Ken knew this arrangement wouldn't hold Donna for long. He blew a sigh of relief when she acquiesced.

While exercising, she decided to study the mystery list Thea Germaine had loaned Jim, along with the official list of victims as printed in the Johnstown Tribune of July 31, 1890, fourteen months after the flood. She was glad she had purchased several historical writings about the flood while visiting both the museum and the memorial so she could make the comparison.

After her conversation with Jim, she had several days to consider whether the placement of a list of the dead under Thea Germaine's office door every May 30th for all these years deserved further examination. It was an odd occurrence. What she was looking for, however, remained a puzzle.

She spread out the copy Jim forwarded to her and then opened one of her books containing the official list. Doing an initial cursory review of the two, she considered them to be exactly the same. Only on mile two of a five-mile treadmill routine did she examine the two lists more closely, comparing the lists as to where the dead had been buried. Each list was the same, listing Grand View Cemetery, Sandyvale Cemetery, Lower Yoder Catholic Cemetery, Saint Mary's Cemetery, Old Catholic Graveyard, German Catholic Cemetery, and the Public Plot.

In addition, there was a list of those whose remains were buried out of the area or out of state, a list of those for whom there was no cemetery record, and a list of those who were not known to have been found. There was even a miscellaneous acknowledgement of those who had been taken for burial, but were listed from the location where they were found dead. Each list appeared to be the same.

She was stumped. Someone had gone to a lot a trouble to type an identical list. There must be more to this. Donna continued her examination. About to give up near the end of her fifth treadmill mile, she spotted it. Her excitement almost caused her to fall off the exercise machine. She took another look. Yes! This had to be it. The official list from the newspaper counted two thousand two hundred nine dead. The typed list counted two thousand two hundred ten dead. One more had been added! But who?

The hunt was on. The Pit Bull side of her had been engaged. She quickly showered, ordered Chinese take-out for Ken to pick up on his way home, and went immediately to her office. There, line-by-line, she painstakingly compared both lists. Into her second hour, with her neck and shoulders tight from tension, Ken appeared.

"What are you up to?" he inquired, giving her a kiss.

She quickly shared the latest developments surrounding the mystery list.

"You found one more name?"

"Not exactly," Donna confessed. "I found one more number added to the official list. Instead of it being twenty-two hundred and nine, the dead on the new list is twenty-two hundred and ten."

"A typo?" Ken questioned.

"That's where I went at first, but I'm haunted by the fact this list keeps showing up, year after year with no explanation."

"You would have thought the Johnstown Museum people would have looked into it years ago."

"To tell you the truth, I don't think they saw the discrepancy in the numbers. I almost missed it myself."

"Is this related in any way to the Croaker case?"

Donna deflated. "I don't think so. It's just something Jim sent to me."

"You'll probably find a typo."

"The reason for it appearing all these years?"

"People do crazy things, Donna. Believe me, just when I think I've seen it all, something pops up that boggles my mind. This could be nothing more than some little old lady who thinks she's contributing to the events surrounding the yearly acknowledgement of the flood by leaving a list of her own under the door."

Donna sighed, suddenly exhausted. "You're probably right. I just need to finish my examination, just to be sure."

"You're okay if I eat then before it gets cold?"

"Sure. Pick out a good movie for us on TV and I'll join you with my dinner in a while."

Donna continued her pursuit, doggedly examining each line for a discrepancy. Page after page yielded no results. Whoever typed the mystery list had the endurance of Job, she thought. Her eyes were growing tired, and her back was aching from hours of concentration. Discouragement was finding subtle entry into her resolve. Suddenly, she stopped and looked, and compared again. She circled the entry, not daring to lose her place. Moving on to the rest of the list, she finally completed the comparison to her satisfaction. She returned to the circled entry, holding her breath. And there it was!

Lacy Sue Larson returned to work after an extended maternity leave. Saddened to part with the twins, she was heartened by the fact Gavin and Carole would be watching the two while she and Saul were at work and Mary was in school. While she knew they were in capable, willing, and loving hands, she had a taste of being a stay-at-home mom, and loved it.

The first thing she noticed upon her return was the added security at the front and back entrance of the assisted living center. She questioned her supervisor, who simply replied there had been an incident and they were enacting enhanced security measures. Lacy Sue remained puzzled. She surmised something more was afoot. Within the hour, Heather Blaine, the front end nurse, clocked in and Lacy Sue knew all she needed to know. She immediately headed to Doris Lewis's room, and found her asleep. She noted the strange photo on the nightstand. Apparently, Doris was adamant it was not to be removed.

Lacy Sue examined the photo while Doris slept. The man staring back at her had an evil smile. She was starting to put the pieces together. Lacy Sue had noticed Gavin and Carole seemed rather tense in recent weeks. They had surrounded their property with added security measures. Gavin was especially antsy, checking his cell phone often. She overheard Gavin asking Ken about Donna's security. Now she understood. Donna was in trouble. The woman who had patiently guided her back to her own sanity was in trouble. If it weren't for Dr. Donna and her own husband Saul, she would now be dead, or completely insane.

She continued to study the photo. She knew the eyes of evil when she saw it, and they were staring back at her.

Chapter Fifteen

Jim Callahan was in a funk. Not a thing was going his way and he was becoming increasingly frustrated. Nothing he did seemed to produce results. Not his efforts on the Croaker case, or his research into the death of Judge Reeder, or the mysterious yearly typist of the Johnstown Flood death list. Maybe he should have stayed in South Carolina.

Just as he was at the peak of self-pity, his iPhone registered a call from Donna DeShayne.

"Why are you callin' me on a Sunday night?" he asked. "I hope you have good news for me, gal, 'cause I have nothin' on this end."

"I don't know what I have, that's why I'm calling."

"Back up, girl, and tell me what this is all about," Jim said in his usual slow Southern drawl.

"The list of the Johnstown Flood. That's what I have. I think I found something!"

Donna then went on to share her diligence in separating the official list from the mystery list.

"Okay. Go slow and tell me this again," Jim said, already encouraged.

"It's a good thing you guys don't pay me by the hour, that's all I can say. I compared the two lists. They are identical until we get to the section, 'Not Known to Have Been Found.'"

"And?"

"And…the list is substantial! However, the official list yields an interesting omission."

"And that would be?"

"Under the 'Rs', there are five Rosenfelt names. Last name only. No first names.

"Okay. Why should I be impressed?"

Donna smiled broadly before she spoke. "You should be impressed because the typed list names a sixth Rosenfelt. First name Julia!"

Jim was stunned. "What does it mean?" he finally asked.

"I don't know. It could be someone is trying to tell us the official list isn't so official after all."

"Okay, be that as it may, why, after more than one hundred twenty-five years, is this an issue and one mentioned only in the last twenty or so years?"

"Jim, you are asking questions I have already asked myself."

"Did you check to see if this Julia Rosenfelt was buried in one of the local cemeteries and this is a simple clerical error?"

"That was the first thing I did. But no, she is not listed in any other category."

"So now what?"

"I think we need to call the cemeteries and ask if they have a plot for a Julia Rosenfelt, death May 31, 1889.

Jim and Donna divided up the local Johnstown cemeteries. Jim took Sandyvale, Lower Yoder Catholic, and the Public Plot. Donna took Grandview, Saint Mary's, Old Catholic Graveyard, and the German Catholic Cemetery. Each agreed to contact the other with any news. They understood Julia Rosenfelt might have been interred out of state, in which case, they might never know what became of her.

Donna began her search the following morning with the lesser-known church plots. When each administrator was informed it was an official investigation, they were more than willing to cooperate, but explained it would take time to go through the records. By the end of the day, all three had called to report there was no listing for a Julia Rosenfelt. That left Grandview Cemetery. When Donna contacted the cemetery the following day, she was directed to its administrator, Trudy Zimmerman.

"Dr. DeShayne, this is Trudy Zimmerman. How can I help you?" she asked cordially.

Donna had not shared the existence of a mystery list with any of the cemetery personnel. "Ms. Zimmermann, thank you for taking my call. I'm interested in knowing whether there is a plot for a Julia Rosenfelt at Grandview. Her death would have been May 31, 1889."

"The day of the Johnstown Flood," came the subdued response.

"Yes."

Zimmerman was immediately curious. "We don't often get calls for those who died more than one hundred twenty-five years ago. Is this a research project, may I ask?"

"Why, yes it is," Donna replied, feeling secure in her response.

"As it turns out, Dr. DeShayne, we do have a Julia Rosenfelt interred here at Grandview. Her plot is in the far corner of the cemetery. The headstone lists the date of death as May 31, 1889. The reason I know this is because for as long as I've been here, and that's been just over twenty-five years, flowers appear on her grave every May 31st. Not only on her grave, but at the Monument of Tranquility overlooking the Unknown Plot of seven hundred seventy-seven graves. They are delivered by a local florist. We've never been able to determine who is responsible for their placement and believe me, we've tried. Even the florist doesn't know. We've never been able to trace payment back to the sender."

"How interesting," Donna replied, her mind going in a hundred directions. "Tell me, has any attempt been made to determine whether or not Julia Rosenfelt had a family?"

"A limited attempt. Most records were destroyed in the flood. There was a rush to bury the dead to prevent disease. Proper records were not kept, I regret to say. I took it upon myself some time back to do some research and came up with nothing."

Donna decided to go for broke. "Mrs. Zimmerman, are you aware that Julia Rosenfelt is not listed on the official record of the dead?"

There was a long pause before the caretaker answered. "I am aware of that fact, Dr. DeShayne, although I have kept it to myself for years. I simply concluded the omission was a clerical error. Remember, it was a horrendous time, and mistakes were made. Many of them, in fact. Some bodies were so unrecognizable guesses were made as to their identity. In a few instances, families were so desperate to find their loved ones they claimed a body beyond recognition just to have someone to mourn and bury. Shock and denial were rampant. Graves were hurriedly dug to prevent the spread of disease and temporary markers were placed. Whether those markers represented each of the dead correctly is another question all together."

"I understand," Donna said quietly, unnerved by the sheer honesty of the administrator. Another thought entered her mind. "May I ask whether you know a Mr. Bob Boykin?"

"Everyone knows Bob. Why do you ask?

"When I visited the Grandview the day after the fundraiser for the Johnstown Museum, I spotted Mr. Boykin across the cemetery, but when I made an effort to approach him, he disappeared."

"That sounds like Bob. He was probably doing some follow-up work for our groundskeeper. Bob is somewhat reclusive, though highly capable and a near genius. You should know many of us are descendants of flood victims."

Donna noted the shift in the conversation. "You are a descendant of a flood victim," Donna said rather than questioned.

"My great-grandparents are buried here at Grandview."

Donna shivered before asking, "And Mr. Boykin?"

"Bob and I went to school together. He, too, is a descendant." Donna heard a deep sigh from the administrator before she continued. "Dr. DeShayne, you may appreciate that oftentimes trauma from one generation can be transferred to the next generation, and maybe even the next. The flood brought with it a whole generation of post-traumatic stress disorder victims before the term became vogue. Don't forget, the flood happened less than twenty years after the Civil War. Our nation was still healing from a brutal self-inflicted confrontation and its aftermath. Gettysburg was fought less than one hundred twenty miles from Johnstown. The region was still healing from its loss of husbands, fathers, brothers, and lovers."

Donna didn't quite know where Zimmerman was going with her dialogue, but understood there was a message.

"Mrs. Zimmerman—"

"Please. Trudy will do fine," the administrator offered.

"Trudy," Donna began slowly, invoking a quiet tone, "I agree transgenerational PTSD exists. A great deal of research has been done on the subject of post-traumatic stress symptoms being passed biologically to the next generation and the next, with each generation being less capable to cope with stress. Children of Holocaust victims, and the World Trade Center attack are just two examples of the possibility. Children of slaves sold away from their parents, or black husbands and black wives sold away or brutalized are another. Sexual and physical abuse are other examples. Not every generation is vulnerable, mind you."

"I'm pleased to know you are so well informed, doctor. When it comes to Bob Boykin, I suspect he has been generationally challenged in this respect. We've maintained our friendship since school days, and while he can be rather reclusive and suffer from bouts of extreme anxiety, I am proud to see how well-respected he has become through it all. Just my personal opinion, mind you."

"I have taken enough of your time, Trudy. On my next visit to Johnstown, I will look you up. Perhaps you can show me the burial site for Julia Rosenfelt."

"I'll surely do that."

Donna found the conversation with Trudy Zimmerman odd, even going out of her way to explain Bob Boykin. Now why did she feel the need to do that? Satisfied she had located the final resting place of Julia Rosenfelt, however, she placed a call to Jim Callahan.

"Good for you!" Jim exclaimed when Donna reported she had located the grave of Julia Rosenfelt.

"I don't know what good it does, though. It doesn't get us any closer to our serial killer."

"We seem to have bits and pieces of a puzzle that may fit or not," Jim lamented. "I did manage to uncover an interesting tidbit, however."

"Is it good?"

"I can only use the word 'interesting' for this one. When I looked further into the missing art piece from the auction, I stumbled on the fact George Heiser secured a loan against it several years ago."

"A loan? What does this mean? One would think after such an opulent display at the fundraiser he was using his own money."

"I agree. It may explain why he was so antsy when I last visited Thea Germaine regarding the mystery list. I don't know why he would have to borrow against something so valuable. I have a lot to learn about the ways of the wealthy."

"Is this the only piece in his collection collateralized?"

"I don't know yet, but I'm certainly going to find out. I learned one can borrow money using valuable art as collateral. The interesting thing about this is you can continue to keep possession of the collateralized piece."

"So that's why he could 'auction' this particular piece at the fundraiser."

"Exactly. Now, the challenge when one does this is to ensure the information about the piece serving as security against a loan does not get out. If it becomes public knowledge, the risk of the art piece being devalued is multiplied."

Donna pondered the implications before speaking. "It makes you wonder how many of the other pieces auctioned off that night were subordinated."

"It does. If more than one was involved, you can bet our Mr. Heiser uses several different auction houses in the transactions. Apparently, each transaction of this nature bears language guaranteeing anonymity. He wouldn't want word of this to leak out, I'm sure."

"Then how did you find out about this one?"

"Through our investigation into Judge Reeder's death. We asked for the judge's files going back five years to determine whether anyone he dealt with had reason to kill him. In the course of our review, we came across George Heiser's file. Heiser used Reeder as a go-between in the loan transaction, setting up a limited liability corporation as the primary owner of the art piece."

"Is that legal?"

"Perfectly. It protects the real owner from being identified, especially if Heiser is not named as a primary owner."

"The corporation is the owner."

"Precisely. Our George is no fool. He had a separate written agreement with Reeder outlining additional terms to secure his continued ownership. There's still much we don't know about this transaction."

"Or George Heiser for that matter."

Chapter Sixteen

"Hey, girlfriend. I haven't heard from you in a couple of days. Everything all right?" Carole inquired of her friend in an early morning phone call.

"As good as can be expected. I feel like a prisoner in my own home. It's starting to get to me. Fortunately, I have a full schedule this week at the office. It'll help take my mind off of things. How are the babies?"

"They get cuter every day! Mary is so protective. She gets after us if we allow them to cry a bit longer than she thinks we should. Say, its Gavin's birthday on Friday. Any chance you and Ken can come by to share birthday cake with us?"

"Oh, I almost forgot with everything going on. Sure. Count us in."

"Great! I bought him this sexy cologne. It's called Contours."

"Is it new?"

"I think it is, but I bought it because I love the name as well as the scent. That man can contour my body at any time."

Donna smiled at Carole's often referenced comments on their sex life. Carole and Gavin were proof sex often gets better with age. In their case, however, according to Carole, it never waned.

"Back up. I haven't had my coffee yet."

"Sinful. See you Friday."

Friday brought with it a thunderous storm toward evening while the group was enjoying birthday cake and admiring the children. Despite the periodic crack of thunder, the festivities didn't miss a beat. Donna and Ken surprised Gavin with a gift card to a local gun range, knowing he was a gun enthusiast who often went to the range to practice. It was a holdover from his days as an FBI agent. Saul and Lacy Sue presented Gavin with a new set of barbecue utensils and an exotic spice set. Mary was excited to give her own gift with help from her parents. It was a new teal-colored golf shirt. Carole was the last to present her gift of cologne. "Now you can smell nice while you're barbecuing, shooting, and playing golf," she said before kissing him sweetly. He immediately opened the cologne to smell, rubbing a bit of it on his arms.

It was soon time to leave. Donna, though enjoying her friends, had not mentioned she was getting another headache toward the end of the evening. It *had* been a grueling week. The extra sleep over the weekend was just what she needed. Something, however, was etching at her memory, but she remained elusive as she hugged her friends in farewell. Perhaps with extra rest it would come to her.

Calavacchi was gathering his data. Every move his ex-wife made was observed and photographed. He was amused by the extra security. She was never left alone, as if that fact could stop him. The fools! They obviously underestimated him. His history as a ruthless, unforgiving despot had apparently been forgotten. Had they forgotten the threats after his sentencing? Or the testimony by experts during his trial who determined he was a runaway sociopath and a danger to society? The others he didn't care about, unless he needed them to accomplish his goal. For now his focus would remain on the good doctor. He had a score to settle.

Gavin called Ken the second he got word Chance Larson had committed suicide in prison.

"Are they sure it was a suicide?" Ken asked.

"It's the initial report. If it wasn't a suicide, it was made to look like one. Calavacchi would have every reason to have Larson offed. He was a loose end. I doubt Calavacchi had any warm feelings toward the man who gave him his first hint of where his ex was."

"I can't say I'm sorry he's gone. He was a parasite. Nonetheless, Saul and Lacy Sue will have to be told. I'd like you to be there when I break the news."

"Try to keep me away," was all Gavin said.

Later that evening, Ken and Gavin made a visit to Saul and Lacy Sue to tell them of the death of Chance Larson. There was little response or reaction from the couple.

"To tell you the truth, my father has been dead to me for a long time. I never made any attempt to contact him once he was arrested, although he wrote me numerous letters from prison,"

Saul shared. "It's better that he's gone. I'll call my brother David to let him know, though there is no love lost on David's part where it concerns our father, I can assure you."

Lacy Sue simply nodded her consent at her husband's comment, holding her husband's hand in loyal devotion.

The diary was taken down from the top shelf in the closet and read. Again. The reading had become a ritual over time. It would help reinforce resolve and commitment. The details were explicit, the tragedy complete. Strangers, nameless faces, foreigners, tramps, traveling men, passengers on board trains, visiting country people, all had fallen victim with the residents.

The children. Always the children. Three hundred ninety-six less than ten years old would perish. Ninety-eight children would lose both their parents. Whole families were wiped out. A family of eight. Another of ten. Another of twelve. And the list went on. Wives lost their husbands and their children. Husbands lost their wives and their children. Some of the dead were not found until weeks or months later. Fifteen in July. Another thirty in August. The fall yielded another crop of dead. For years to come the bodies would turn up.

The survivors, racked by grief, despair, and fear, sought refuge anywhere they could. All that belonged to them had been swept away. Any structure that was still standing served as refuge. For miles around not a house was standing. What were they to eat? How would they continue to live among the threat of typhoid fever and famine? It was the night that brought the greatest fear. The dark. The remains of the dead were still waiting in the dark. Many would wait for a very long time, with decaying flesh of both animal and human filling the lungs of the survivor.

It wasn't long before the thieves came to plunder and loot. Robbing and pillaging their way, anything that could be carried off was done so without a whim of guilt. Even the dead were stripped of their possessions. Who was going to stop them? The poem in the diary had been read many times.

Many thousand human lives—
Butchered husbands, slaughtered wives.
Mangled daughters, bleeding sons,
Hosts of martyred little ones
(Worse than Herod's awful crime.)
Sent to Heaven before their time.
Lovers burnt and sweethearts drowned,
Darlings lost but never found!
All the horrors that hell could wish,
Such the price that was paid for—fish!
A dam, which vomited a flood
Of water turning into blood:
A deafening, rumbling groaning roar
That ne'er was heard on earth before;
A maddening whirl, a leap a dash—
And then a crash—and then a crash—
A wave that carried off a town—
A blow that knocked a city down.
All the horrors that hell could wish,
Such was the price that was paid for—fish!
An hour of flood, a night of flame,
A week of woe without a name—

A week when sleep, with hope had fled,
While misery hunted for its dead;
A week of corpses by the mile,
One-long, long week without a smile,
A week whose take no tongue can tell,
A week without a parallel!
All the horrors that hell could wish,
Such was the price that was paid for—fish!

—"The Price of South Fork Fish" - Issac G, Reed, 1889

Who was going to pay for the atrocities visited upon the people? Someone had to pay. There had to be a day of reckoning.

The research had been done. The plan was being perfected. The details. It was always in the details. Another contrived day of reckoning would surely unfold. It was the only way.

Donna holed up in her home office for most of the day, pondering the events surrounding the Croaker case. She added to the existing timeline the death, date, and photo of Judge Reeder as well as the appearance of the mystery list each year. Stepping back for another look, she puzzled whether the two were connected in some way. The fact Julia Rosenfelt was an addition to the official list was disconcerting, but the explanation offered by Trudy Zimmerman was plausible. A simple mistake in the original count. Yet, why was someone so intent on drawing attention to the error year after year? Why, after all this time, did the museum not simply amend the official list to include Julia

Rosenfelt? Then again, what purpose would it serve to amend it? Doing so may even enable another mystery list with another name. No, it was better the museum left well enough alone, Donna determined. They knew what they were doing.

Then there was the matter of the frog pin appearing on Judge Reeder's robe at the time of his death. Who had such close access to the judge to afford such an opportunity? Donna decided to call Jim. He answered on the third ring.

"I thought I would check in to see how the interrogations are coming along on the guests at the fundraiser," Donna said.

"We're just about finished. I hope to have a printout of the anomalies in a couple of days. So far, the greatest issue remains the catering and grounds people who have not yet been identified. We plan to single that group out for greater scrutiny. By the way, George Heiser is up in arms upon discovering we are asking questions about his loan history regarding his artwork and other valuable acquisitions. He's threatening to sue for breach of privacy."

"Can he do that?"

"He can, but whether it will stick is another matter. I think it's more posturing than anything else."

"This doesn't sound like our 'Gentlemen George'. He could be hiding something and asking questions about his financial affairs makes him nervous."

"I thought of that. Time will tell."

"Has there been any progress on determining who had access to Judge Reeder's robe the day he was killed?"

"None. We've questioned everyone he was in contact with that day and rechecked their declarations as to where they were and what they were doing. Their stories hold up. The judge entered his office at about 9:15 AM. His legal assistant brought in a cup of coffee along with the case under current consideration shortly thereafter, reminding him he was to meet with the other judges later in the afternoon before writing an opinion brief. There was no other reason for his assistant to return to the judge's office nor was he summoned. At about 10:45 AM, the judge was seen at the copier and then returned to his office. He was late for his 11:00 AM court appearance, which was unusual for him, as he was known to be prompt. They waited about fifteen minutes before going to his office, only to find the judge slumped over his desk. He was dead. The box of chocolates was on his desk. Four of the six were missing."

"He was wearing his robe?" Donna asked for confirmation.

"He was. The assistant said he usually put it on first thing and never took it off until the end of the day on most occasions. It usually hung on a coat stand behind the door."

"The cleaning people and maintenance people were also questioned, I assume."

"You would assume correctly. The security people, the parking attendant, the chauffer, everyone. I can see why this case had Russ Carotti so frustrated. It's a nightmare. All roads are dead ends."

"We're going to get a break, Jim. I won't rest until we solve this thing. At some point our killer is going to make a mistake."

"We can only hope."

Chapter Seventeen

Donna focused on creating a spreadsheet on the twenty-two murder victims. She entered the place, age, and date of death, as well as the gender, the poison used, and the approximate time it took for the death to be determined as intentional. It took her most of the day to compile the information into a more readable format other than her office wall. She studied the printout for a couple of hours before calling Jim again.

"Hey, what's up?" he asked.

"I'm emailing a spreadsheet to you I created on the murders. I haven't found anything useful, but I was curious as to the dates of death. Are the dates provided by Russ the actual day of death, or the date the body was found?"

Jim was stumped. "I just assumed they were the dates the bodies were found. I never considered they were actual dates of death. That would make a difference. Should I ask Russ?"

"Let me see what I can do from this end. I can always get a copy of the death certificates. It will take a while, but it will be worth it."

"Let me know what you find out. In the meantime, I'll study the spreadsheet."

The flaw in Donna's protection plan was the mailbox. Calavacchi was delighted by the discovery. He observed the couple had to cross a county-maintained road to retrieve mail on the other side of the street. In doing so, they crossed the perimeter of protection. All he had to do was wait until the good doctor went to the mailbox. It was only a matter of time.

He was thoroughly enjoying the hunt. After all these years, she was still beautifully curvaceous, and far more alluring with a shorter auburn-colored hairstyle, a departure from the long, flowing blonde hair when they were married. She had matured nicely, no longer girlish in her manner, but provocatively woman-like. He liked that. What it could have been like if she had not betrayed him. He remembered the early years. He had known he had to have her the minute he'd laid eyes on her. She was so young and innocent. So naïve and malleable. So incredibly captivating. She would have done anything for him. How he liked showing her off to his business associates. He dressed her, dined her, bestowed untold jewels upon her, and bedded her to his complete satisfaction. He knew others ogled her from a distance, not wanting to be obvious or offensive to the boss. They dared not come close, but secretly they were envious.

Things started to go awry when she wanted a baby. No way was he going to have this innocent masterpiece of a woman deformed by pregnancy, or have a crying baby interrupting their love-making. Besides, he was in the midst of building an empire.

He was on top of his game. Anyone who got in his way was vanquished. He was building a reputation. He was the twenty-first century version of Lucky Luciano, his hero.

It was never the same again after she'd announced she was pregnant. He demanded she have an abortion. She cried and pleaded with him for reconsideration, but he was adamant. He wanted her all to himself. No way would he share her tits with a suckling kid! It was then he lost her.

He had years in prison to think about the consequences of his decision as he stared at her photo in his cell. A baby would probably have saved him from this hell hole. If she were busy with a kid she may not have betrayed him by transferring his computer files onto a memory stick, turning it over to law enforcement. It was the act of a woman scorned. He had lost not only his woman, but his empire. His empire he could redeem. His woman he would kill for her betrayal.

Did she not understand? How had she misinterpreted the signals? He'd grown up in the ghettos of New York. His Italian father and Irish mother fought constantly. He and his brother, Carl, grew up hungry most of the time. They'd huddled together against the lack of food and attention, determined to stay together. Neighbors fed them when they could, mindful the parents were dysfunctional and disengaged in the affairs of their sons. Eventually, their father killed their mother in a drunken rage and he was sent to prison. The boys ended up roaming the streets, parentless, homeless, and desperate for food. It was always the hunt for food. Then the law of the street took root in Donald. The older brother would become the leader, and Carl would be the follower. Every day they had something to eat, and a place to sleep because of Donnie.

Carl saw Donnie change before his eyes. He saw the hate in his brother's scowl. Often Donnie would say there would be a time when never again would he or his brother be hungry. Never again would they not have a home. Donnie became a legendary street fighter, never wavering or showing weakness. He stole, he lied, he became whatever he needed to be to live and thrive, and he would take his brother with him on the journey. Before too long, Donnie had provided a place of their own, a place no one could take away from them. And there was food. Plenty of food. And hot water. Not to mention girls. Donnie loved the girls, and they loved Donnie.

There were times when Donnie would disappear, but show up days later. When Carl asked where he had been, Donnie always replied, "Been checkin' the streets for business." Carl knew not to question further. The bond between the brothers was like cement. The loyalty intact.

And then the unthinkable happened. Carl was dead, killed execution style. A rival gang was responsible. Donnie collapsed in utter despair, completely unglued by his brother's death. It was some time before he gathered strength, and when he did, he would begin a reign of ruthless revenge and never looked back. Never again would someone take something precious away from him. In a matter of months, every member of the rival gang was dead. Retribution was sweet. Yet, the longing for love was insatiable.

Shortly thereafter, Nichole Lewis crossed his path as a guest of a guest at a poolside function. She was incredibly beautiful and alluring. Immediately smitten, he found his way into her heart and panties in record time. In short order, he decided she was the woman for him. It was a whirlwind romance, and he pulled out all the stops.

He knew her upbringing was lackluster, at best. Her mother divorced her father years ago, and raised Nichole as a struggling single parent with two jobs. While she attempted to give her daughter every advantage she could muster, the effort was meager by his standards. He was determined to right the wrong.

Donnie and Nichole soon became an item. Business associates who wanted to curry Calavacchi's favor took notice. Nichole was showered in gifts and acts of recognition. She was the candy on Donnie's arm and no one was about to ignore the obvious. The boss had a lady. A very beautiful lady.

They soon married in a lavish affair on a cruise ship in the heart of the Caribbean, beyond the scope of prying eyes. It was a seven-day affair. Donnie took extra effort to make Nichole's mother, Doris, feel especially welcome. Still Donnie's eyes wandered. Even on his wedding ship, he would take any women who offered herself to him. Enough was never enough with Donnie. It was not only the lack of food in his youth, but the lack of love in his heart. For the rest of his life, he would seek love. It was usually found in his bed. Nichole would be the last to know. Her innocence would be her undoing, but not for long.

After the abortion, the dynamics between the couple shifted. Nichole was crushed and immersed in a depression that slowly evolved into unbridled anger. Vacillating between a young girl's brain and a women's need for choice, she slowly morphed into a vitriol foe against her own husband.

Donnie couldn't help but notice her distance. He showered her with more attention and gifts than ever before, but to no avail. She remained aloof both in and out of the bedroom. Trying to convince himself she would get over it, he secretly feared he was losing her. She was no longer his "little Nichole," the innocent, naïve young woman he married. She spoke far less and began to take notice of everything. It was then he made the decision to step up security. The order was given; she was never to be left alone.

In a casual, off-beat comment, Donnie mentioned to Nichole about the added security he had put in place. His explanation to her was that he was entering into a delicate phase of his business that might anger a lot of his business associates when he eventually succeeded. He assured her the added protection was temporary. She absorbed the information without comment, knowing it was useless to object. Nichole understood she was being contained, guarded, and corralled, and anything she said or did would be reported to her husband. Her friends had stopped coming to visit, scared off by the goons watching over her. Except for her neighbors, Carole and Gavin Tandermann, who took an instant dislike to her husband from the start, there was no one to talk to. Her mother visited infrequently, and when she did, Donnie always made it a point to be present. Ever the gracious host and doting son-in-law, he would arrange for Doris to go on vacations and trips at his expense for long periods of time. He even purchased for her a house, paying all expenses to ensure his mother-in-law did not move in with them. He thought of everything, except Nichole's eventual betrayal that would send him away to prison. She would come to regret her choice. He would see to that.

The death certificates of the Croaker victims were coming in slowly, some online and others by mail. Donna tacked each one to her office wall, matching them with the information and photos already posted. She decided she would study them later the next day.

"If I would have known you were going to cover this wall with all of this, I would have had it corked," Ken said jokingly as he entered her home office just as Donna stepped back toward her desk.

"I can see spackle and a paint brush in your future," she returned with a giggle. "Oh, speaking of paint brushes, the Tandermanns want us to come by the coffee shop in the morning to give our opinion on a proposed redo of the interior of their shops. They hope to build their brand by making all the Beans cafés look alike. I thought it might be fun. What do you think?"

"Sure. Besides, who could resist free coffee and pastry?"

Ken was pleased to see Donna more herself. The strain of looking over her shoulder, since Calavacchi's escape had begun to take a toll. She was looking haggard from restless nights and uncertain days. The Croaker case was serving as a distraction, despite the lack of progress, and Gavin and Carole were doing their part in diverting her attention to other events or family matters.

The next morning, Ken and Donna arrived early at the coffee shop only to find it already mobbed. Carole and Gavin waved them over to their table.

"You definitely need to enlarge this place," Ken said, looking at the patrons still working their way through the door.

"Or find bigger digs," Gavin replied.

For the next hour or so, Gavin and Carole shared their objective for a planned interior and exterior design to each of their cafés. They had done their homework, and the designs were not only impressive, but inviting. Donna and Ken were not decorators or design people, but they knew a good thing when they saw it and encouraged Gavin and Carole in their overall scheme.

Carole checked her watch. "I want to catch the cleaners before they close. They're only open half a day on Saturdays. I also promised Lacy Sue I would pick up diapers and formula. I've gotta' run." She kissed her husband and friends before heading toward the door.

Donna, however, perked up at the mention of the cleaners. She vowed to call Jim with her question.

She was growing more excited as she perused the wall. Bingo! She found a pattern, but had no idea what it meant. Even so, it was something, a small break. It was late, but the growing sense she had stumbled on a vital clue was overwhelming. She placed the call.

Jim answered on the fourth ring. He sounded groggy, as if he were asleep. "Donna? What's up, girl? What time is it? Ken okay?" It was obvious he was struggling to get traction.

"I am *so* sorry for calling so late! It simply can't wait 'til morning. I think I found something!" Donna replied, her voice at pitch level.

"Give me a minute to get to the kitchen. I don't want to wake Karly," Jim returned slowly.

Donna was beside herself waiting for Jim to come back on the line.

"Okay. Now what's all the excitement about?" he asked groggily.

"You remember I promised to gather the death certificates of our twenty-two victims in the Croaker case?" Donna started by way of introduction.

"I remember," was all Jim said, still trying to shake the sleep from his brain.

"I have half of them in, and posted them to my wall."

"Good for you. This would be important, why?"

"Because," she said, her voice gathering strength and conviction, "the eleven death certificates all show December 31st as a date of death."

Jim remained quiet, not daring to speak.

"Did you hear me?" Donna fervently questioned.

"Donna, forgive me. I've had a hellish week. Karly insisted I take a sleeping pill before going to bed early. I think I register you have stumbled onto something, but for the life of me I'm not able to decipher its implications. Can I call you back in the morning? By my third cup of coffee I'll be able to take on anything."

"Oh, Jim, forgive me. Ken often says when I latch onto something I don't let up. Go back to sleep. Call me in the morning."

The phone call ended, but Donna's racing thoughts and conjecture would, for her, rule the night. She got out of bed in the wee hours of the morning to look at the wall in her office, looking for clues. She was onto something, she was sure of it.

Mid-morning, Donna took a call from Jim. Normally she would have slept late, this being the weekend, but not this morning. She was keyed up.

"Okay, beautiful. I'm all yours. Give me everything you've got," Jim said in his slow Southern drawl.

"There are two things," she began, methodically. "First, did anyone think to determine whether Judge Reeder's robe was at the cleaners?"

Jim was stumped. "That would be important, why?"

Donna could tell Jim was not in the mood for guessing games. "Judge Reeder's robe was discovered with the frog pin. Was it at the cleaners before his death?"

"I simply have no idea, but I don't see how that is important. So the judge is wearing a clean robe. How is that relevant?"

Donna noted Jim's tone was somewhat vexed. After all, she'd gotten the man up in the middle of the night. She had better deliver.

"It's not the cleaning that would be important, but the access to the cleaning. Could someone have planted the pin on the judge's robe in the cleaning process?"

It was then Jim was struck with the clarity of the question. "It's possible," was all he said at first. "Yes, a real possibility! How else could the pin have been delivered?"

"I think it bears looking into. There's another thing, however, that is far more vexing. As I mentioned last night, I've been gathering the death certificates of our twenty-two victims. I have eleven so far."

"And?"

"And...all eleven of them have the date of death as December 31st."

There was silence on the other end of the phone.

"You've got to be kidding?"

"No. I'm looking at the results right now. I am still awaiting the other eleven, but if the pattern holds, we have a killing six months before the anniversary of the Johnstown Flood each year. Except in the case of Judge Reeder."

"Why a departure with the death of Judge Reeder?"

"I can only guess something accelerated our killer's schedule. Maybe the Croaker is up against the clock and has to speed up the killings. Or perhaps there's been a life-changing event that would alter the schedule."

"Or it can simply be a fluke."

"I don't think it's a fluke. Our killer is too methodical, too predictable. Whomever it is, wants to be discovered."

"How do you figure?"

"I wasn't sure at first, but the death certificates, the presence of a pin on each of the victims, and possibly the revised list of the dead from the flood that shows up on the 30th of May each year all point to a purposeful pattern. Whomever is doing this has been laughing all these years."

"We don't know the revised list of the dead is related to the Croaker case, though."

"No, we don't. I've got a feeling it is, however. Call it woman's intuition."

Jim was thoughtful before he spoke. "Do you think our killer has changed course and plans to double the killings?"

"Because Reeder was killed in June and not December? Are you thinking there will be another in December?"

"It's a thought."

"God, I hope not."

Chapter Eighteen

He watched and waited, as he had done every day for the last eight days. He was determined to invest whatever time it took to complete his objective. Parked a safe distance from the house he was confident his truck would not be seen or recognized. Upon later inspection, a pile of cigarette butts would mark his hiding place.

Then it happened. He watched Donna leave her home and walk across the side yard to the other side of the road to retrieve mail from the mailbox. My, but she was beautiful! He was salivating at the thought of the reunion about to happen. It was long overdue.

Using the distraction, he stole his way out of the woods, across the side yard straight toward the front door, all the while making sure her back was turned away from him still studying the postal delivery. He was careful to open the front door so as not to make a sound. He was grinning from ear-to-ear. Now all he had to do was wait for her to return.

The boyfriend had left early that morning. It was sheer stupidity to think a simple perimeter monitor could thwart his plan. By the time the boyfriend got there, she would be dead. In the meantime, he would have his way.

Donna entered the house, still peering at the mail, tossing some in the trash, while opening others. She stopped. The scent was familiar. It was then she was grabbed from behind in a throat-lock, cutting off oxygen.

"It's been a long time, Nichole," the voice from behind said. "It's nice to have you back in my arms again."

The day had dawned. There was no mistaking the sound of the sinister voice, the brutal force, or smell of his sweat. "You've been a bad girl," he continued in a swarthy manner, while she gasped for air. "You did me wrong, girl. After all I did for you, you did me wrong. I don't forget a betrayal. I wish it were someone else and not you."

Donna's self-defense courses kicked in. She wasted no time, elbowing him in the stomach and stomping as hard as she could on his foot. The grip around her throat loosened as he yelled in pain, allowing her the seconds she needed to wrestle free.

Catching a glimpse of her ex, she saw his face laced in rage. She regretted not having carried her gun as Ken had urged her to do, and it was now out of reach. She turned to flee out the back door. She was almost down the steps when she heard the door behind her open. A second later she was tackled to the ground, the weight almost crushing while her arms were pulled back roughly, hands tightly tied behind her back. It was then that she was turned over to face her past. Depravity stared back at her.

"Ever the lone warrior you are, Nichole. Tsk. Tsk. I'm looking around for your security. I guess he took the day off. When are you going to learn I always get my way?"

"You piece of shit! What do you want from me?"

He smiled maliciously. "You have to ask? Surely, we were married long enough for you to learn I always have the final say. Or have you forgotten my promise at my sentencing? Now, I'm going to take that pretty face of yours and make it unrecognizable. You will definitely need a closed casket."

Reaching into his back pocket, he retrieved a knife. "Do you like it? I bought it just for this occasion. It will be one-time use only, Nichole...or Donna...or whatever you are calling yourself these days."

"Donald Calavacchi! This is the Horry County Police Department. Throw down the weapon and step away. We have you surrounded!" the microphone blared. Donna recognized Ken's voice.

Calavacchi smiled down at his ex-wife, clearly enjoying her discomfort as she shook uncontrollably. "Looks like the cavalry has arrived, my sweet." And, with that, he pulled her to a standing position, using her as a shield, the knife positioned at her throat.

"I wouldn't be too hasty there, cowboy. You see, I can slit this velvety throat in half a heartbeat. She'll bleed out in seconds. Now, here's what we're going to do. I'm going to walk the good doctor to my car, and you're going to let me leave. Make no mistake. She's going to die. It's either she dies today, or tomorrow, or the next day. It's your choice, cowboy."

"You're crazy if you think we're going to simply stand by and let you take her. If any harm comes to her, Calavacchi, you will come to regret it," the microphone blasted.

"I've been threatened by the best of them, cowboy, and I'm still standing."

Just then, three shots rang out. Calavacchi's eyes rolled back in his head. His face registered shock before wavering in a futile effort to maintain balance before finally collapsing forward to the ground, the weight of his body once again crushing Donna. Ken rushed forward, his gun drawn. He kicked away the knife, felt for a pulse to be sure the escapee was dead, and retrieved a gun holstered at the man's ankle before extricating Donna from her entanglement. She was covered in blood that was not hers. Once he untied her hands, he took her in his arms, holding her tightly, as she sobbed. It was then he looked around.

The gunshots were a surprise. He knew they hadn't come from him. He looked at Caleb Blackwell questioningly. Caleb shook his head. The other three officers securing the scene had the look of disbelief as they looked beyond Ken and Donna. Ken turned to see what they were looking at, only to find Gavin walking slowly and speaking softly. When Gavin reached his objective, he placed a gentle hand on the shoulder with imploring words.

Donna looked up at Ken to find his attention diverted. She followed his gaze.

"Oh, Ken! No! No!" She stood up immediately, but Ken held her back.

"Donna, let Gavin handle this. Please, honey," he pleaded.

Gavin slowly and soothingly took hold of the shotgun from shaking hands. It was cocked and ready to fire again. He disengaged the hammer. One of the officers stealthily came beside Gavin to relieve him of the weapon, wisely stepping back after doing so, assessing a yet-volatile situation.

"It's okay. Everyone is safe now. The danger is gone. Donna is safe and with Ken."

"Safe," was the only response.

"Yes, Lacy Sue. Donna is safe."

Donald Calavacchi was dead. Examination would reveal the escaped prisoner was shot three times from behind, one shot taking out the upper part of his head, spewing brain matter and blood all over Donna. Ken at first thought Donna had been shot as well, but when she moved and groaned under the weight of her ex, he was relieved to find the only casualty was Calavacchi. The other two shots were wasted. Calavacchi was already dead before their arrival.

Gavin enfolded Lacy Sue in a fatherly, protective embrace, as he walked her slowly back to her home, just up the street from Ken and Donna's place, while delivering soothing words of comfort. Gavin phoned Carole while they walked, careful not to add to Lacy Sue's fragile state. Both Carole and Saul were in the yard waiting for them, their faces laced in horror as the babies slept through their nap. Mary was at school, but would return in another two hours. Gavin suggested to Carole that she go to Donna. He and Saul, he assured her, would manage until her return.

Ken, still trying to comfort Donna, directed Caleb Blackwell to call for both an ambulance and the county coroner. Each arrived within minutes. The paramedics attended to Donna first, assuring Ken she was not injured, just badly shaken. The dead man was transferred to the ambulance and driven way. Donna was directed by Ken to sit in the back seat of his county-issued vehicle, allowing the door to remain open so he could keep a close eye on his beloved. Ken was fully engaged in securing the scene, but his attention was divided between the needs of Donna and the unexpected event involving Lacy Sue.

"I want to see Lacy Sue. I want her to see I'm okay," Donna called commandingly to get Ken's attention, exiting the vehicle.

"Not if I have anything to say about it," Carole Tandermann announced upon her arrival beside the car. "Lacy Sue is being cared for. You, my friend, need a shower and a drink, not necessarily in that order. I, for one, am going to start us with a stiff drink. I suggest you join me. And Ken," she yelled to the detective, "I'll have something waiting for you."

"Bless that woman," Ken said to himself. Carole and Gavin were always there when you needed them.

Carole, hovering over her best friend, laid a sporty outfit on the bed for Donna to wear after showering, all the while watching her friend carefully for signs of distress. Although a retired psychiatrist, the doctor side of her was highly alert to the effect stressful situations could produce.

After her shower, Donna dressed slowly, and then sat on the bed, suddenly overcome by fatigue.

"You okay?" Carole asked softly.

Donna took a moment to respond. "It's over. It's finally over," she said in a subdued tone. "All these years of looking over my shoulder, waiting for him to pounce, and here I am with it all behind me. To think it was Lacy Sue who would be my liberator." Overcome with emotion, Donna cried. Carole came to sit beside her friend, holding her in a protective embrace.

"You cry as much as you need to, sweetie. You have sixteen years of making up to do. That bastard took a chunk out of your soul, but not your life. You have friends and family, Donna, who love you very much. Nothing can hurt you now. Nothing."

Hours later, Ken texted Gavin to say he and Donna were on their way. Donna was anxious to see Lacy Sue. Gavin met them on the front lawn. Never one to be chatty, Gavin enfolded Donna into a prolonged embrace before ushering her into his home.

Lacy Sue sat in the sunroom with little Carole asleep in her arms. A cup of tea sat on the coffee table. Saul, grateful for the support, hugged Donna first and then shook Ken's hand. Saul looked scared. He was concerned Lacy Sue would relapse. Donna placed her hand on his shoulder before sitting down beside Lacy Sue.

"It's going to be okay. She's stronger than she looks," Donna whispered to her former patient's husband. Saul sat down quietly across from Lacy Sue.

Ken was proud of Donna. She was determined to support her former client and friend, despite the trauma to her earlier in the day. They both sat on the couch on either side of Lacy Sue.

"What are you having, Lacy Sue?' she asked innocently, eying the cup of tea on the coffee table.

There was a slow response. "I think Saul made me peppermint tea. My favorite. A touch of honey works best."

"That sounds delicious, and just the thing I need right now. Saul, would it be asking too much for a cup of my own?" Donna asked. Saul quickly headed to the kitchen after transferring little Gavin to Carole, looking over his shoulder toward his wife before leaving the room.

Gavin hovered in the corner of the room, while Carole took little Gavin and placed him in his crib. Moments later, she came back to take little Carole from Lacy Sue to put her in her crib as well.

Donna looked at Lacy Sue for any sign indicating shock and found none. Her former patient was not trembling, or fidgety, nor were her eyes darting about. If anything, she looked surprisingly calm and collected.

"You're worried about me," Lacy Sue said. "You are all worried about me. I can see it in your eyes. Saul is beside himself. How do I let him know that I'm okay? I am finally okay!"

Donna stole a glance at Carole before responding. Carole shrugged slightly. Donna signaled for Gavin to get Saul. She suspected this was something he should hear.

Donna leaned in toward her young friend, placing her hand on Lacy Sue's knee. "Tell us why you are finally okay, Lacy Sue." Saul and Gavin were in the doorway listening.

It was some time before Lacy Sue spoke, and when she did, she lifted her head, taking on an air of assurance. Her eyes betrayed not a hint of fear.

"I've been watching things lately. Gavin and Carole installed added security around their home. You and Ken did the same. That told me something was wrong. Gavin was especially antsy, but tried to hide it around Saul and the children.

"When I saw the photo of the man with the evil eyes on your mother's beside table, I knew my suspicions were right. On a day your mother's memory was more available, I questioned her about the man in the photo. It was then I learned your real name. An Internet search told me all I needed to know. As you know, the trial was in all the New Jersey newspapers at the time. I was able to download the articles."

Donna sat stunned at Lacy Sue's revelation. Everyone in the room was stilled by her accounting.

"I continued my research and discovered Donald Calavacchi recently escaped from prison. I surmised his escape was the basis for the added home security and for the big fellow who shows up every morning at your home. I figured he was personal security. You see, I have a direct line of vision from my home to yours from my living room window.

"In recent days, there was a black truck parked off the road, hidden by trees. It was either you had hired additional security or you were being watched. I used my high-powered telephoto camera lens to zero in on the make and model of the vehicle along with the license plate and discovered it was a rental. I knew then you were being watched. In my mind, it was unlikely local security would be driving a rental car."

"You were watching the watcher," Ken said, getting up from the couch to have a look into the living room at the picture window. In all of his visits to their home, he never once noticed the Larsons had a clear view of his front yard.

"Yes. The thing I discovered was a flaw in your home security," Lacy Sue continued. "Yours as well," directing her comments at Gavin and Carole. Gavin paled. In light of his former role as a district security supervisor for the FBI, this was not welcome news.

"You see," Lacy Sue continued, "when you are both home, the system works well. As programmed it allows for two people to pass the protection threshold at specified times during the day. When only one of you is home, however, it still allows for two people to pass the perimeter. You were never given a code to adjust from two persons to one person. Your ex discovered this as well. When he observed you going to the mailbox, he knew he could enter the property without setting off the alarm.

"The fact you relied on personal security from your home, to your office, and then home again was another flaw. There was no guard outside your home, only the security system."

"How did you come to have such knowledge of security systems?" Gavin asked, clearly rattled by his young friend's summary.

"I figured it out. I don't know how, I just did. Fortunately, last week and this week I am scheduled to work nights, allowing me to keep a watch on your front yard from my living room window, figuring your ex would make his move when you were home alone, which is always in the morning."

Donna glanced at Ken who simply shook his head in disbelief. "I didn't have to look over my shoulder. You were doing it for me," Donna said while squeezing Lacy Sue's hand.

Lacy Sue continued her monologue. "This morning the truck was again in the woods. It arrived especially early. I got a bad feeling and hardly left the window. That's when I saw Donna go to the mailbox, crossing the perimeter. She retrieved the mail, but lingered at the box, looking through the circulars. In no time, a figure came stealthily across the side yard and entered the house. I recognized the face from the photo on your mother's bedside table.

"By the way, I videoed from the moment you went to the mailbox. I stopped when he entered your home."

"Why didn't you call me?" Gavin asked incredulously. "You shouldn't have gone alone."

"I wasn't thinking. I just knew I had to do something to save you," Lacy Sue confessed, turning to her former doctor with teary eyes. "After all you have done for me, I couldn't...wouldn't let anything happen to you."

Donna, choked with emotion, looked up at Ken who had tears in his eyes as well.

"Where did you get the gun?" Ken asked gently, struggling to stay composed.

"I gave it to her for Christmas several years back," Gavin shared with a tremor in his voice.

Carole, who had been quiet all this time, went to her husband's aid. "Gavin would take Lacy Sue in the early days of her recovery to the shooting range, giving her lessons on how to handle, shoot, and maintain a firearm. We hoped it would give her more confidence, given her history."

"Yes, I remember now," Donna offered. "I thought it was a good idea."

"I kept it in the gun safe and took it out only when I went to the range for practice," Lacy Sue explained. "When I saw the guy enter your house, I retrieved it from the safe. It was already loaded. I was on automatic pilot. It's the first time in my life I have ever been so focused. I texted Gavin and Ken before heading for your home. I planned to enter from the back door, hoping it was not too late.

"It was then I heard the commotion at the back door. By then, Ken and two other patrol cars arrived. I stayed hidden behind the bushes fixed on the entire scene. When I heard him vow he was going to kill you, something snapped in my head. It brought me back to the insane look in my ex-husband's eyes when he threatened to kill me eleven years ago. I was weak and powerless then. Someone else had to save me from his insanity, and they did. I wanted to be that person for you, Donna."

Everyone was watching Lacy Sue carefully. Something was different. The resolve was evident, the loyalty for her friends unmistakable.

"How do you feel, now?" Donna ventured forth, still probing, ever the doctor.

Lacy Sue turned her head to look at her husband, lovingly. Saul was crying, the tears streaming down his face unabashedly.

"My husband has been my rock all these years. I have been gifted with the love of all loves. Each of you has supported me in my journey and I am so very grateful, but now it's time I be there for all of you. I have sat here for the last several hours feeling strangely liberated. I finally took charge. For the first time in my life. There was no other choice, of that I am sure. I did what had to be done. I hope you can understand."

Saul approached his wife and knelt, placing his head in her lap. She stroked him with an air of absolute devotion, drawing him to her. It was such a private moment, Donna rose and signaled for everyone to leave the room. They gathered on the front porch, deeply moved by transpired events.

"The liberated becomes the liberator," they heard Carole say.

CHAPTER NINETEEN

The transformation in both Donna and Lacy Sue was unmistakable, each for different reasons.

Donna, after sixteen years of hiding her true identity, felt an inner honesty leading to an incredible feeling of personal freedom. It allowed her to be more focused on the Croaker case now that her former husband was no longer a threat.

For Lacy Sue, her metamorphosis resulted in an air of self-assurance and confidence. No longer was she the fragile, mousy woman of eleven years ago. Almost immediately, she evolved into a woman of substance, so much so that within months of the death of Calavacchi, Lacy Sue was promoted to head nurse at the assisted living center with a substantial pay increase, a welcome turn of events with the addition of two more to their family.

Both husbands were elated by the changes taking place in their wives. While Saul was building his landscaping business, Ken, on the other hand, was keeping a secret.

The prosecutor's office, in their review of the killing of Donald Calavacchi, had not yet cleared Lacy Sue of murder, despite the fact she had been called in to give an accounting of the incident, of which Ken, Caleb, Gavin, and the other two officers at the scene collaborated. It had now been eight weeks since the killing and the prosecutor had yet to rule.

That evening, while playing cards with the Tandermanns, Ken decided to unburden his concern while they took a break to have cake and coffee. The conversation turned, as it often did, to Mary Larson and her new siblings.

"So this morning, Mary was feeding her baby brother cereal. When she picked him up to burp him, he spit up all over her shoulder. The look of horror on her face was priceless," Gavin shared. "We had all we could do not to roar with laughter."

"She's quite the little mother. Always hovering, making sure they get the attention they need," Carole added.

Donna looked over at Ken who remained quiet. "You okay? You don't seem yourself tonight."

He leaned back in his chair, placing his hands on the table. "I'm worried about the prosecutor's delay."

"What do you mean?" Donna asked. Up until now, Ken had never mentioned anything about the prosecutor since Lacy Sue's appearance at his office.

Gavin understood immediately. "You mean they haven't cleared her yet?"

Ken shook his head.

"What do you mean they haven't cleared her?" Carole asked her husband. "Cleared her of what?"

Both men hesitated in their response. "Murder," Ken finally said.

"What? Murder?" Donna volleyed, shocked by Ken's comment. "Don't tell me she can be charged with murder! That's absurd!"

Ken held up his hands. "Now, let's not go there. It usually doesn't take this long to render a decision, that's all I'm saying. There could be a perfectly good reason for the delay; something totally unrelated to the case. I'm just antsy for this to be put to rest."

"You never said anything. All this time I thought the matter was resolved," Donna responded forcefully.

"What's your position, Ken? Can they levy a charge?" Gavin asked, attempting to defuse the tension.

Ken sighed. "The killing would have to be viewed as a justifiable homicide."

"What's the ground rules for that?" Carole asked, clearly agitated.

"Generally, they would have to determine the killing was committed without malice or criminal intent, and that it was committed in self-defense, and/or in the defense of others, or while trying to prevent a serious crime, or in the line of duty.

"Most of the time, when it is committed by a citizen, it has to be determined if the citizen had reason to believe that a serious crime is about to take place, or is taking place, or that such action was needed in self-defense."

"So where's the problem?" Donna countered. "Clearly Lacy Sue determined a serious crime was taking place."

Gavin came to Ken's rescue. "I think Ken is concerned because Lacy Sue shot Donald Calavacchi from behind."

"So?" Carole said, her eyes darting back and forth between the two men.

"So, it may be viewed as pre-meditated," Ken explained.

"Oh, for Pete's sake!" Donna fired back.

"This is crazy!" Carole jumped in, now fuming. "You mean if Lacy Sue and Calavacchi were face-to-face and then she shot him we wouldn't be having this conversation right now? Something like, 'Excuse me Mr. Calavacchi for interrupting your plans to murder my friend, but I have to blow your head off now! So would you turn around so I can shoot you in your face?'"

Gavin put his hand on Carole's shoulder, signaling her to calm down. "I think we should all go back to our corners and just wait for the ruling. In the meantime, I'm having another piece of cake."

Ken and Donna flew to New Jersey for a long weekend with Ken's daughter, Megan, her husband, Greg, and their newborn, little Kenneth. Grandpa Ken was in his element, enthralled by his grandson and proud of Megan and Greg in their newfound roles as parents. Both parents and baby were thriving.

While at the Bishops, Donna took a call from Jim. "Sorry to bother you on the weekend, Donna, but I thought you would like to know that we checked out the cleaners where Judge Reeder's robe was cleaned and came up with nothing. No one recognized or saw the pin. The clerk on duty the day the robe was checked in said the judge's wife brought it in for cleaning and came back several days later to pick it up again."

Donna tried to hide her disappointment. "So the pin was not attached to the robe in the cleaning process, nor did anyone on the judge's staff have access to the robe. His family doesn't have a clue where the pin came from and never saw it before. This is frustrating. Our killer had just enough access to apply it to the robe. How?"

"If we knew the answer to that, we would most likely know who our killer is and be able to solve this thing."

A hint of autumn was in the air. The temperatures were becoming more pleasant after a scorching summer. Thanksgiving would soon be upon them. Donna reflected how it had been over a year since being invited by Jim to assist in the search for the mysterious serial killer they had named the Croaker. While some progress had been made, it wasn't nearly enough. And to make matters worse, another killing would occur at the end of December if the timetable Donna had put together were to hold true. The only anomaly in the pattern was the killing of Judge Reeder at the end of June, a departure from the killer's usual methodic path.

Carole was to come today for lunch, bringing samples of flooring she and Gavin were considering for their cafés in their attempt to harmonize the interiors of their stores to look the same. At one point they entered Donna's office to retrieve her eyeglasses.

"Whew! My, but you have a strange decorating style," Carole said, looking at the photos on the wall of the twenty-two victims.

"Very funny. I didn't expect them to be hanging here this long."

"How are you coming with all this?"

"Painfully slow, I'm afraid. We have established a pattern, however."

"Tell me."

Donna proceeded to unfold the pattern of the killings she discovered.

"Now let me get this straight. At first you thought you had the dates of death, right?"

"Yes. The copy of the file Jim gave me turned out to be not the date of death, but the date the body was discovered. That's what threw us off. Once the discrepancy was corrected we were able to see a pattern."

"How odd. The good news is your killer is obsessive to the point of being ritualistic," Carole said offhandedly while still examining the photos.

"My goodness! I hadn't thought of that. Do you think this is part of a ritual?"

"It might be given the appearance of the pin and the consistency of the deaths being at a certain time of year."

"Yet something interrupted the order of things with the death of Judge Reeder."

"It appears so. You will only know for sure this coming December. If another body shows up, the killer is back to the original timeline."

"You are the consummate bearer of good news," Donna teased her friend.

"I try."

The following week, Ken called Donna excitedly. "Call Carole and Gavin. We're going out to dinner tonight. We're celebrating."

"What's the occasion?"

"Lacy Sue was exonerated in the shooting of your ex. The video she took helped a great deal."

"Oh, Ken! That is cause for celebration. It's a good thing we never told Lacy Sue or Saul of our concern."

"That was a sleeping dog we didn't need to kick."

Chapter Twenty

The home of the Tandermanns' was once again filled with the aroma of foods of every description in observance of Thanksgiving. Three highchairs were added to the dining room table to accommodate the babies born to friends and family during the year. Large platters of turkey, stuffing, potatoes, and gravy found their way around both the adults' and children's tables, followed by lasagna and ham and multiple offerings of vegetables, breads, and cranberry sauce.

The room was humming with conversation and laughter, adorned in every manner of blessing as was so obvious in the toasting that went on through dinner as each guest agreed to share his or her favorite blessing of the year.

Lacy Sue got the biggest round of applause as she so eloquently recited her reasons for gratitude and thanksgiving.

Jim and Karly, as well as Jeff and Julie West, joined the festivities with Jeff regaling everyone with tales and jokes. It would be another memorable occasion.

The next day, Ken and Donna hosted a sumptuous brunch at their home for friends and family. It was agreed everyone would arrive at 10:00 AM for a spectacular offering of French toast, omelets, sausage, bacon, and potato cheese soufflé, along with various juices. Of course, cereal for the kids and for those who didn't want French toast or eggs was available. Carole was assigned the coffee detail. Gavin brought up the rear with breakfast pastries.

The ladies, including Mary, planned to spend Black Friday Christmas shopping while the guys babysat the three infants and the Blackwell's two sons, Paul and Samuel. Donna, Carole, Lacy Sue, Mary, Julie, Megan, and Sienna loaded themselves into two vehicles and headed to the outlets, but not before giving the guys directions in the care and feeding schedule of the babies.

They shopped for a couple of hours and then met up for lunch across the highway at Olive Garden. "You would think with all the food we've eaten in the last two days, we wouldn't be hungry, but I'm starving," Donna announced to the ladies.

"It's the shopping," Carole said while digging into the large salad bowl. "Spending money takes a lot of energy."

"Why does spending money take a lot of energy?" little Mary Larson asked her grandmother with a look of confusion.

"Because I have to fight them from prying it from my hands," Carole replied, enjoying her granddaughter's bewildered look.

"Oh, Grandma! We can't take you anywhere." Everyone laughed heartily.

After lunch, the ladies returned to the outlets to pick up where they left off. They agreed to meet at the pretzel shop toward late afternoon before heading home. Everyone broke into teams, with Lacy Sue, Mary, and Sienna headed in one direction, Julie and Megan heading in another, and Donna and Carole teaming up for a few additional items.

"I'd like to hit the fragrance shop to check out the latest in men's colognes," Carole announced to Donna as she headed in that direction.

"Didn't you give Gavin cologne for his birthday?"

"I did, but I'm not crazy about it. It was okay at first, but it's gotten dull."

"Well, we can't have dull, can we?"

"Nope. I try to avoid dull at all cost," Carole quipped.

They entered the shop and were immediately hit with a cornucopia of scents and fragrances. Donna was dubious about staying too long given her sensitivity to certain smells. Nevertheless, she entered the shop and explored the offerings, taking a brief sniff now and then. She picked up a small canister and sprayed it in the air. The scent was familiar. She concluded it must have been the one Carole purchased for Gavin for his birthday. Within minutes, she felt a headache coming on, a sure sign she had stumbled across cologne she was allergic to.

"I'm going to step outside and wait. Take your time," she said to Carole. Her friend simply nodded, engrossed in her search.

Donna sat on a bench in the sun, enjoying its warmth. Within minutes her headache began to dissipate. The fresh air was working. Before long, Carole exited the shop.

"Find anything?"

"No. I think I'm hooked on good ole' Old Spice."

"Can't go wrong there," Donna returned while checking her watch. "We've got a few more minutes before meeting the girls."

"Then let's head to the kitchen store. There must be some little gadget Gavin or Lacy Sue doesn't have."

They quickened their pace and headed toward the kitchen shop. Donna was feeling better, left with only a small lingering discomfort behind her eyes. Something, however, was nagging at her memory. Where had she smelled that scent before?

Donna spent Saturday in her home office pouring over facts and figures on the Croaker case. She and Jim agreed it wasn't going to be much of a holiday season if the killer struck again.

Deciding to examine each of the victims more thoroughly, she first began to create another database. There was a reason why the killer chose all of these people. A common theme connected them all. She was determined to find out what it was.

She entered the name of the victims in the order of their date of death along with the city and state of death. Then the names of their parents, the city and state of birth, and the date the body was discovered was entered. Lastly, the method of poisoning and the poison used, their professions, and the name of the husband, wife, or nearest next-of-kin along with their contact information. Setting up the database took her all of Saturday and most of Sunday morning.

Examination then began on the first three victims. She reasoned if she discovered a notable consequence in the first three victims, it just might hold true for the remaining nineteen. It was worth a shot.

Isolating the first three victims revealed some interesting information, but nothing earth-shattering. The first, John Barrett Symington, was born and raised in Arizona, having established a law practice in Scottsdale. He was forty-seven years old at the time of death. This she knew from an earlier conversation with Jim.

The second victim, Raymond Richard Jarrett, was born and raised in Virginia. He was a financier with a large banking concern in North Carolina. He was fifty years old at the time of death.

The third victim, Peter Max Wellons, was found in South Carolina, but was born and raised in Pennsylvania until his graduation from Penn State University. He was a housing contractor of considerable presence in the Charleston area until his death at the age of forty-nine.

Doggedly, Donna continued her review by downloading and comparing obituaries on each of the first three victims as well as a general Internet search. She discovered all three were successful businessmen of standing in their communities in both wealth and prominence. Were the wealthy being targeted? she asked herself. Or prominent business people?

Somewhat encouraged, she isolated the next three victims in the same manner as the previous three. Again, this next group were of known wealth and stature. One was a state representative in Maryland, another was a surgeon in Charleston, South Carolina, and the last was a restaurant owner in New York. All three had been born and raised in other states.

Donna was so intent in her review she did not hear the door to her office open.

"I know that look when I see it," Ken said, placing a kiss on her head.

"Oh, you're here. Be a dear and rub my shoulders," she begged while trying to work the kinks out of her neck.

"You've been at this for hours. Are you coming to bed?"

"What time is it?"

"It's nearly eleven o'clock. Even Pit Bulls need their sleep."

"I think I'm onto something." She shared with Ken her findings.

"You've done six so far," was all he said after she finished. "You've been working on this for two days with sixteen more victims to go," he continued while massaging her neck and shoulders.

She sat back and sighed, suddenly exhausted. "You're right. I need to go to bed. Oh that feels good," she purred, closing her eyes, while Ken did his magic.

"There's more where that came from," he whispered alluringly.

"You sure know how to get a gal's attention. Take me to your leader!"

The next morning, Donna was up before dawn and again in her office. Ken presented her with a cup of coffee at 7:00 AM.

"Oh, you are so good to me," she said reaching for the cup he placed on her desk.

"After last night, it's the least I can do," he returned with an engaging smile. "Are you going to be at it all day?'

"Yes, and for the foreseeable future, for sure. I don't see any other way. I'm fairly certain there will be another murder by the end of this year if we don't crack this thing."

"Just so you know," Ken said, kissing her before heading out the door on his way to work, "you're my one and only."

"Right back at 'ya, babe," Donna returned endearingly.

By mid-afternoon on Wednesday, she pulled away from her desk, not daring to breathe. She looked again to recheck her findings. Standing to work out the kinks in her neck and back, she stretched, permitting her body a respite from its intense concentration these recent days, all the while keeping her eyes on the computer screen.

"Maybe, just maybe," she said to herself, still pacing the floor.

In the 'What, Why, Where, When, and Who' investigative scenario, she knew the 'What', the 'Where,' and the 'When.' It was the 'Why' and 'Who' that remained elusive. Until now.

The pieces of the puzzle were crowding her brain for placement, so much so she had to steady herself as the waves of understanding and insight took hold.

"Of course," she said satisfyingly. "It makes perfect sense. Now all we have to do is figure out the 'Who.'"

Chapter Twenty-One

Jim called Donna the next day with an update on the interrogations. "I have good news and bad news," he announced.

"Give me the good news first."

"The good news is we have tracked down and interviewed most of the catering people, bartenders, orchestra people, and wait staff on duty the day of and before the fundraiser."

"Most of?"

"That's the bad news. There are still three we have not accounted for. We hope to have them identified in a couple of days. Now, here's the thing. Some of the wait staff and bartenders, men and women, were used to assist people from their vehicles onto the carriages, which necessitated changing their clothing from footmen to waiters and back again when the carriages took everyone back to their vehicles at the end of the evening. It was these footmen who gave out the boxes of chocolates as people stepped down off the carriage."

"So it's possible one of these footmen could have been our killer."

"I'd say it's probable."

"My God! This person was in our midst all evening! For all we know they could have served us our drinks and appetizers!"

"A chilling thought, but true."

Donna had another nagging thought. "Tell me, did the guests have to park their own vehicle before boarding the carriage?"

"No. I'm told their cars were seen to by parking attendants. Why?"

"So no one who drove to the fundraiser had their car keys during the affair."

"Not until the attendants returned them at the end of the evening. What's bothering you?"

"I don't quite know," Donna admitted. "Too many loose ends and too little time, I guess."

Donna wasn't quite ready to share with Jim the results of her work these last several days, for reasons even she couldn't explain. She needed another day or so. Her instincts were now on high alert. Engaged in a race against time, she sensed the storm of justice about to turn in their favor. If she were wrong, there would be another victim.

Christmas Eve found Ken, Donna, and the Tandermanns at Saul and Lacy Sue's home. Lacy Sue was eager to entertain her friends and family this year by providing a light dinner before everyone gathered around to sing holiday songs. Then they opened gifts. Mary and the twins were a delight to watch. The twins and their big sister sat in the middle of a circle of adults who showered them with their wish list. It was such a special evening, but Donna's mind was elsewhere. She almost felt guilty for having a good time while the clock was ticking on another anticipated murder by the Croaker.

Gavin was on his hands and knees putting together a small train set for the babies. Mary was close by, handing Gavin the pieces.

"You smell good, Grandpa. I like your old aftershave better than the new one Grandma got you for your birthday."

Donna, overhearing the comment, smiled and then froze. Something triggered her mind to a distant memory of little consequence at the time. Now it came flooding back against a backdrop of swirling thoughts. She suddenly stood, her face white as a sheet.

"Donna, what's wrong?" Ken asked, quickly coming to her side. The others looked in her direction.

She remained frozen in place, staring straight ahead, her face taking on all manner of expression as if transported to another realm.

"Did I say something wrong, Aunt Donna?" Mary said with a look of concern.

Hearing her niece's tone of uneasiness, Donna immediately gathered her wits and knelt before the little girl, hugging her tightly.

"No, Mary, you did nothing wrong. In fact, sweetheart, you may have just saved the day."

Mary looked confused, but turned to her grandpa to continue assisting with the train track. Gavin looked up at Donna, but said nothing.

Donna rose to her feet, taking Ken to the side out of earshot from the others. "I've got to call Jim. Now."

Ken took on a knowing look. He had seen this side of Donna before. "You know who the killer is then."

"I hope I'm wrong, but yes, I think I do."

It wasn't much of a Christmas Day for Donna or Jim. Donna's phone call the night before had sent the Pittsburgh detective into a tailspin. It took a while for Jim to grasp the impact of Donna's assertion. Emailing him her database did the trick. Calling her back after a thorough study and numerous questions, he was now fully on board. They agreed on a course of action to determine the weaknesses and strengths of Donna's supposition, creating a to-do list for the next several days. Time was running out. Knowing this, they spent little time second guessing their assignments.

Donna, in all fairness to Ken given her anticipated absence on Christmas Day and the foreseeable future, gave him an overview of her suspicions and conclusions. He listened intently, asking questions now and again for clarification. When she finished, he sat back in awe of her summary.

"If what you say turns out to be true, you will have solved the crime of the century," was all he said.

"There'll be plenty of time to gloat after we bring an end to the killings. Until then, there is a lot of work to do. I hope it's not all for nothing."

Jim and Donna spoke frequently through the day and for the next couple of days, both buried in researching, using both the Internet and official files. Coordinating efforts with other entities, Jim was able to roll out an outline of action in no time. Donna made numerous phone calls, each one produced information that filled in the blanks, bringing them closer to the killer.

Operation Croaker was about to begin.

In two more days it would be over. Another vindication was near, another long-overdue act of retribution. Requital, once again, would be sweet. This was likely the last. Circumstances had changed, and not too soon. In the final analysis, there was diminished pleasure as the years wore on with little-to-no recognition. The outlet to explain and underscore had not been satisfied. Law enforcement had proved inadequate and inept all these years. How many more signs did they need?

The story must be told. People must understand the personal gestures expended all these years, the sacrifices made, the untold hours of planning to settle the spirit of the departed, a spirit largely ignored. Then recognition would come, and applause. Maybe even tribute.

The people would understand. They would get it. Far too many of them had been on the receiving end of injustice, often thrown to the wolves by politically motivated and weak leaders. The people would see justice could be served, even years later, to right the wrongs, and undo the indolent practices of their leaders.

Perhaps it was time to announce oneself as the perpetrator. The logical sequence in such a revealing would be swift and punishing. No matter. There was another way out, but in the end the people would understand once the truth was revealed. It would be worth it. A lifetime achievement. And then peace would be realized.

Donna flew to Pittsburgh at the urging of Jim three days before the start of the New Year. She asked permission for Ken to join her, and Jim readily agreed, though he would have no jurisdiction. It was prearranged for Donna and Ken to be picked up at the airport by an officer and driven to the investigative unit where Jim greeted them warmly. He then led them to a conference room where several others from the detective squad were already gathered. Introductions were made before discussion began.

Donna learned surveillance had already been placed on the suspect. There were several in the room doubtful of Donna's suppositions. Jim needed everyone on board with where they were going with the plan. He asked Donna to review her findings and conclusions. She was prepared to do this with a PowerPoint demonstration and began immediately going over the facts and figures as she understood them. The presentation took more than an hour. A 'question-and- answer' session ensued.

"I'm not suggesting I have the answers to every last question. I believe, however, we are on a track that must be pursued regardless of the outcome."

"If you're wrong and the real killer gets away?" questioned a member of the team.

"Then we are going to have to face the fact we didn't save Victim Twenty-Three. However, what if I'm right? Are you suggesting we do nothing and just sit on this information? If the press ever finds out we could have saved the latest victim and didn't, they will crucify us and rightfully so," came Donna's commanding response.

"I don't mean to offend, but quite frankly, I find this whole thing rather far-fetched. I just don't want our department to look foolish," the officer returned.

"Then I would suggest you not be involved, if you are worried for your reputation. Personally, I would like to see every one of you fully committed. If you're not, no hard feelings," Donna retorted.

Jim provided the final word. "I agree with Dr. DeShayne. We can always find a replacement, but I need full commitment. Do I have it? Raise your hand if you're in all the way."

They looked at each other, but eventually all hands were raised. Donna sat down beside Ken relieved by the outcome. She hadn't thought there would be reticent posturing from a team member, but she was glad so the line of demarcation was established right from the start.

Over lunch, Jim apologized to Donna for his associate's behavior. "He's a good cop, but a little contentious. I understand he was miffed I got control of the case having been so new to the force. In any event, you put him in his place very nicely. He'll do the right thing, I'm sure."

"I hope so. The last thing we need is to be distracted by office politics."

Chapter Twenty-Two

There was a full moon overhead giving off an almost ghostly aura. The temperature was crisp, to near freezing, serving to heighten expectations. Several of the team were strategically hidden from view and outfitted with infrared night vision goggles with a range of fifty feet. All were equipped with audio transmitters. They waited silently, not daring a single movement to give away their presence. It was nearly two hours before the first crackle of audio was heard.

"A vehicle just pulled into the parking lot," the transmitter relayed. It was nearly midnight. The temperature was now below freezing. The wind had picked up.

The sound of a car door opening and closing could be heard. Footsteps along the gravel lot were recognized as making an approach. All eyes were on the subject approaching to the target area. At one point, the subject stopped, going no further. It appeared efforts to continue were labored and exhausting. After a time, the sound of footsteps continued on, but at a much slower pace before finally stopping. The figure seemed in need of a rest before finally bending forward to place the item on the ground. Standing erect, the head bent forward in a benedictory manner for an extended time in soulful prayer.

Retracing the previous steps, the subject walked for a time before stopping, and again bent forward with an item before standing erect in a prayerful pose. It was then the observers heard a voice.

"It appears we have come to the end of our journey," the subject said. "I am conflicted as to whether to be happy or sad. Both, I should think."

Jim and his team surrounded the subject. Flood lights were turned on, illuminating the entire Grandview Cemetery.

"There is no need for drama. I will give you no cause for action," the subject spoke quietly. "My work is done. It is better this way."

It was then that Donna stepped forward after a nod from Jim. Ken was just behind her. All team members had their guns pointed at the subject. They were ready for any indication of resistance.

"I am sorry for your loss," was all Donna said at first.

"There were many losses. I found great satisfaction in acknowledging them, including my own," the subject returned.

"All these years you've been bringing flowers to honor all of the dead, not just your own."

"There is a lack of remembering. Too much time has passed. The people are forgetting."

"Yes. You took it upon yourself to honor their memories with flowers each year," Donna continued softly, not wishing to disturb the willing dialogue. "How thoughtful."

"I knew you were here, doctor. There was a scent in the air where there had been none on my previous visits," the subject shared in a subdued, but controlled manner.

"Is it why you stopped walking?"

"Not entirely. I tire easily these days."

"You come here once a year on December 31st to deliver two sets of flowers. One is placed at the grave of your great-grandmother, Julia Rosenfelt, and the other is bestowed at the Monument of Tranquility."

"Yes, that is correct."

"The other delivery of two sets of flowers is on May 31st of every year for the same gravesite and memorial on the anniversary of the Johnstown Flood."

"Very good, doctor."

"You honor the dead twice a year. Have you accomplished your goal? A remembering of the dead?"

"More or less. Someone had to do something."

"Your great-grandmother's body was found months after the flood, but the final record has not changed to recognize her as a victim."

"A pity. I tried. Mistakes were made. It was a confusing time. I take no issue with confusion. I took it upon myself to make up for the oversight. It was the least I could do."

"The pins. Very clever to have placed them on each of your victims," Donna continued, clearly wishing not to alienate the subject. "A brilliant move."

"Thank you, but I am not moved by brilliance. I am moved by reconciliation. There has been little of that in these circumstances."

"I understand. The record shows a day or two after the flood, a group of angry men went to the clubhouse to confront the offenders, but found no one. The grounds were abandoned, the overseer fled in fear for his life. To alleviate their frustration, they ransacked the premises. One of those men was your great-grandfather, Ira Rosenfelt."

"Yes. A noble gesture on my great-grandfather's part, I might add."

"Years later, you discovered a diary and a box of pins in the holdings of your father upon his death."

"You have done your homework, doctor."

"The diary was that of your grandfather and told of his relentless struggle for wholeness given that your great-grandfather was severely abusive to him and a remaining sibling after the death of his wife and seven children."

"The catastrophe wreaked havoc on many levels. Our family was just one example. A cascade of reaction rather than response, I fear. Grief can do that to a man."

"Would you care to share your own experience as a child?" Donna ventured gently.

"Bravo, doctor. When they brought you aboard the investigative team, I surmised you were a formidable front. Finally, there was someone who knew the appropriate questions to ask. I will answer your questions, Dr. DeShayne, because I have developed a professional respect for you these recent months."

Donna recognized the need for a complementary stance to further engage the killer in ongoing dialogue. "I have come to marvel at your plan; a plan that has been unyielding in its intent and outcome these last twenty-two years. At some point, you made a decision on your life path. Am I correct?"

"You are correct. To satisfy your curiosity, I will share that I was raised by a highly abusive stepfather. He often beat my mother, as well as my siblings and me. I was the oldest, so I took the brunt of the beatings. I was a thoughtful child. I always asked the question, 'Why?' Why the anger? Where does it come from? Years later, my stepfather died. Cancer. It was an ugly death with no one there to assist in his transition. Sadly, he died alone, without the benefit of family. Family had long since abandoned their alliance, wanting no part of him. In many respects, they were grateful for his suffering. They saw it as payback. I know I did.

"I would come to realize, from a reading of my grandfather's diary, that wholeness does not come from an already broken mold. He was beaten by his father, so my grandfather was beaten. We children were beaten by an angry stepfather. The underlying anger is the common denominator. Do you see?" the killer asked.

"I would agree, but not totally. Some have transcended the denominator," was all Donna said, holding her breath.

"Dear doctor. Some have, but not our family. Our path was written in the DNA. In the vibrational levels of our birth date. All I know is that my mission was clear."

"To avenge the deaths of those in the Johnstown Flood," Donna returned with clarity.

"Yes."

"You did so by killing the descendants of members of the South Fork Fishing and Hunting Club," she stated rather than asked.

"Again, bravo, doctor."

"There were over sixty members of the club at the time of the flood. You began your 'reconciliation' with the original sixteen members of the club. The first sixteen murders were targeted to the descendants of the original members. Am I correct?"

"You are a skillful student."

"But to date, there are twenty-two victims. You didn't stop with the original sixteen charter members."

"No, I did not. The quest for justice was too great."

"I continue to struggle on another issue. Perhaps you can assist me. The original charter members of the South Fork Fishing and Hunting Club did not include Andrew Carnegie. Your first sixteen murders were directed to the descendants of the charter members only."

"Yes, at first. Frick, Ruff, Sweat, Charles Clarke, Thomas Clarke, Fundenberg, Hartley, Yeager, White, Myers, Hussey, Ewer, Carpenter, Dunn, McClintock, and Holmes."

"Did you plan to eventually target Andrew Carnegie's family? He was a very prominent member."

"Andrew Carnegie's family would not have been a target."

"Why the departure?"

The killer sighed deeply before responding. "Andrew Carnegie's only child, a daughter named Margaret, was an innocent party. As you may know, her father married late in life, at the age of fifty-one. Carnegie didn't marry Louise Whitefield until after his mother's death. A strange circumstance, if I might add. Margaret was born four years before Carnegie's death.

"The record suggests Andrew Carnegie never visited the South Fork Fishing and Hunting Club, but rather his nephew did on more than one occasion."

"That would explain why a photo of him and other club members was taken in Pittsburgh and not at Lake Conemaugh. He never visited Lake Conemaugh," Donna concluded aloud.

"I would agree. I would also suggest Andrew Carnegie's membership in the lodge may have been gifted by his business partner, Henry Clay Frick, although I am just guessing," the killer added.

"Carnegie was a generous benefactor to the survivors after the flood."

"Another reason not to target his family. Did you know Margaret had four children?"

"I discovered that fact in my research. May I ask who you were targeting today?" Donna asked, knowing it was already December 31st.

"The great-grandson of a South Fork Club member, George Franklin Huff. Quite frankly, though, I was losing resolve and strength. On the drive over here I was contemplating not going through with it."

"We are still struggling with the placement of the pin on Judge Reeder's robe. Can you help us?"

A sly smile formed on the suspect's face. "Reeder should have died a long time ago. The man was a snake, even without his ancestry bearing membership in the club. He was as dirty as the day is long. I took great satisfaction in his demise."

"How did you manage to place the pin on his robe?"

Again a smile formed. "You've thought long and hard about this, doctor. How do you think it came to find its place on the judge's robe?"

Donna knew she was being taunted and teased. Nonetheless, she ventured forth. "You were a waiter at the fundraiser. You appeared in disguise. No one questioned your presence. You served as a vehicle attendant before and after the affair. You positioned yourself so you could attend to not only Judge Reeder's vehicle, but to the transfer of the box of chocolates. It was then you discovered the judge's robe encased in plastic covering from the dry cleaners hanging on a hook in the back seat. It was the perfect opportunity to apply the pin. No one was watching, and you had the keys to the vehicle throughout the evening. You took a daring chance. You had no way of knowing when he would eat the chocolates. As it turned out, he took them to work with him that Monday morning. He was dead before lunchtime."

The suspect nodded and smiled. "That was my most satisfying kill. A good way to end a successful run, I might add. What day he died was not an issue, as long as he died. How fitting he was in his robe when he breathed his last breath. Justice was finally served."

Donna was unnerved by the dialogue but continued. "Would you care to comment on the painting?" Donna probed.

"Ah. The painting. Another story for another day, dear doctor. Perhaps we can move this discussion to a warmer setting. In the meantime, I have need for the restroom."

In a slight departure, the suspect turned to Donna and bowed in a display of respect. "Do not dismay. I have provided the answers to your many questions. My hat's off to you."

The suspect was then frisked for concealed weapons and accompanied to the cemetery's restroom outbuilding. Two officers stood outside the facility waiting for an exit. In the meantime, Donna and Ken had retraced their steps to their vehicle along the gravel path when they heard the sound of gun fire. There was a rush of pandemonium they could not see from where they stood, but could hear. Donna's heart was pounding. She and Ken remained still, shivering in the cold night air. They waited for what seemed an eternity before Jim made his way up the walkway in the couple's direction. He was pale, his face contorted in disbelief.

Without preamble he announced, "Russ Carotti blew his brains out. He is dead. We never anticipated a gun taped behind the toilet."

Donna looked at her watch. It was nearly 12:30 AM on December 31st.

Chapter Twenty-Three

Donna was still somewhat numb when she and Ken met Jim for breakfast the next morning. They spent the night at a motel in Johnstown rather than at Heiser House at Jim's urging. There were still too many unanswered questions circling around George Heiser.

Donna shivered at the thought of events from the night before. She drew her sweater around her to ward off the chill, a chill that was more of the heart than from the cold weather.

"We've learned Russ Carotti never gave up his apartment in Pittsburgh. His claim of a move to Florida was a ruse. Would you like to be there when we examine it for evidence?"

Donna nodded in agreement. Jim looked at Ken who was keeping a close eye on her. Ken had never seen Donna so unglued. Even after the shooting of her ex she managed to rise above it and soldier on. Not this time. This time she seemed wilted and drained.

"Are you up to it, Donna?" Jim asked.

She closed her eyes briefly before responding. "I need to know why. I guess it's the psychiatrist in me, but I need to know what motivated him to such desperate acts of revenge. Yes, I'm up to it."

"We're looking into his background and doing a thorough search of his file during his time on the force. There's an answer. We just have to find it," Jim said.

Donna nodded before smiling weakly. "Just tell me where and when."

Donna and Ken met Jim and two other officers the next afternoon at the apartment building in Pittsburgh where Russ Carotti had lived for nearly twenty-six years. Though an older complex, it was well maintained and manicured with large, mature oak trees waiting for permission from spring to spread their foliage.

Carotti's two-bedroom apartment was on the first floor of a large three-story brick building with four other units on the floor. The superintendent met them with a key. The entrance way was taped in yellow, indicating a crime scene.

The five of them put on surgical gloves and foot protectors before they stepped into the apartment with Ken and Donna entering last. It was immaculately clean and well appointed. Russ Carotti had elegant taste. Not an item was out of place. There were no dishes in the sink or the dishwasher, no clothes strewn about, no magazines left on the coffee table. The book shelves were lined perfectly in size with books on every subject. Donna noted the numerous books on the City of Johnstown and the Flood of 1889.

There were photos on one of the shelves. Several were of Russ in his younger days as a police officer. Other photos showed him with a woman and young child, or with the woman alone, or the woman with the child. They were displayed almost reverently.

"Do we know who these are?" Donna asked Jim.

"His wife and child," Jim answered solemnly.

Donna turned to Jim. "Where are they now?"

"They're both dead, from what I understand."

"Oh dear. How did they die? Does anyone know?" Donna continued to probe.

"I made some phone calls early this morning to three of his buddies on the force who retired several years before Russ. They all tell the same story. Russ's wife and child were killed in a car accident New Year's Eve twenty-seven years ago. They were coming home from a sleepover their daughter had at a friend's home the night before. A drunk driver plowed into his family's car going at nearly one hundred miles per hour. I'm told they never suffered. They were dead instantly."

Ken saw Donna tear up. "How awful," she said. "He must have been devastated."

"They tell me he nearly went insane. To add insult to injury, the driver was never charged with vehicular homicide?"

"How is that possible?" Ken asked incredulously.

"The charges were dismissed."

Just then, one of the officers interrupted Jim's dialogue. "Detective, you may want to see this," he beckoned from the hallway.

Jim walked toward the officer, who directed him to one of the bedrooms that had been converted to an office. Jim surveyed the top of the desk to where the officer gestured. He then went immediately back to the hallway.

"Donna, you may want to come as well. Something's been left for you," Jim said slowly, his face pale again. "Ken, you're welcome to enter as well."

Donna looked long and hard at Jim's face. He was clearly upset. He stood aside, allowing Donna and Ken to enter the room. The officer again pointed toward the top of a large oak desk.

In the middle of an oversize red desk blotter was a letter. It was addressed to "Dr. Donna DeShayne." Donna took a quick look at Ken before bending forward to read it. It was typed double-spaced, dated, and signed.

Dr. DeShayne:

If you are reading this, then I have been discovered and am now dead.

The killings will stop. My justified work all these years will find a place in the subtle footnote of time. My life has had little meaning since the death of my wife and child all those years ago, so my passing will be of little consequence.

I leave behind the information you seek, the answers for your inquiring and brilliant mind.

I implore you not to judge me harshly. I did what had to be done.

Regards,

Russell A. Carotti – December 30th.

Donna stood upright and turned toward Jim. "I don't understand. Why did he leave this for me?"

"I didn't know it was him," Jim said. "All this time I thought he was one of the good guys. I didn't know." Jim looked badly shaken.

Ken turned to the other officer in the room. "May we have a minute?" The officer looked in Jim's direction. Jim gestured a dismissal with his hand.

Ken closed the door to the office, not wishing the conversation to be overheard. "If I'm understanding you, Carotti would call for updates on the case and you would share the latest information."

"I didn't know," Jim repeated in anguish.

Donna came forward, putting her hand on Jim's arm in a gesture of comfort. "None of us knew, Jim. Not until very recently, and even then we were guessing. You can't blame yourself."

"He knew how close we were getting. He could have run and we would never have solved this case."

Donna thought a bit before responding. "I don't think he would have run. He needed the world to know what he had done. He set you up, along with everyone else connected with this affair. It was a brilliantly contrived scheme that lasted twenty-two years and if my guess is right, he took control of it right from day one and didn't let go until he killed himself."

Donna then noticed a long table to the side of the room. It was filled with papers, tablets and journals. Some of the journals looked very old. She picked up what appeared to be the oldest, and gently leafed through it, instantly recognizing it as a diary. Everything was placed in the order of the dates they were written.

"This must be what he meant in his letter about leaving behind information," Donna said. "Russ Carotti was a very precise man."

There was a note in the middle of the table, typed double-spaced, dated, and signed in the same manner as the previous one.

Dr. DeShayne:

You will find everything in order. Each item is numbered in the order they should be examined.

Regards,

Russell A. Carotti – December 30th.

"He oversaw everything, right down to his own death and the eventual investigation," Jim said in awe.

"A master planner," Donna replied, somewhat chilled by two notes left for her by the killer in as many days. "He never planned to kill today."

"What do you mean?" Ken probed.

"He dated both notes December 30th. The killings all took place on the 31st. of December," Jim replied. "Is that where you're going, Donna?"

"It is. He wanted this to end with our finding him at the cemetery. He wanted to die on the same day his wife and daughter died."

Donna continued looking at the items on the table, occasionally picking up one and leafing through it. "Jim, would it be possible to have all this shipped to me so I may thoroughly examine them?

Jim hesitated. "They are evidence." He paused. "We can certainly arrange for them to be shipped, but there is a need to protect the evidence, even though our killer is dead and will never be brought to trial. So here is what I can do. I'll arrange for each item to be copied and catalogued. We can provide you with copies after you sign off on each page. It'll be a little work, but I'm sure we can accomplish our goal. I'll get my guys started right away."

Chapter Twenty-Four

Donna and Ken were met at the airport by Gavin and Carole upon their return to Myrtle Beach. Carole noted how haggard Donna looked.

"Happy New Year, you two! You both look like something the cat dragged in! Temporarily, of course!"

Gavin raised his eyebrows at his wife's remark. "What Carole is attempting to relay is that we've been worried about you."

"They know that," Carole retorted. "I've always been the bull in the china shop."

"We love you for it," Donna returned, hugging her friend.

"Rough trip, I gather?" Gavin probed.

"Very unsettling," Donna replied. "At least there will be no more murders."

"She needs some rest, lots of it," Ken commented while retrieving their luggage from the carousel.

"There are still too many loose ends. I need some processing time," Donna shared.

"Let's get you both home, then," Carole said jovially. "My Gavin put together a chicken casserole and tossed salad for your dinner tonight. It's in your fridge. I restocked with milk, eggs, cheese, and bread. There are some lunch provisions and soup for tomorrow as well. A couple of bottles of wine await your palette. By the way, you were shamefully low on coffee. Not anymore!"

Donna and Ken were overwhelmed by their friend's ministering. "You guys are the best in the world."

"I like to think so," Carole replied with a wry smile while linking her arm with Donna's.

The fatigue had set in with a vengeance. Donna realized it was more emotional than physical. She slept late, getting up for a bagel, but in a couple of hours returned to bed. Entering the kitchen late-afternoon, Donna found Ken had left her a sandwich and a note.

Be back soon. Went to the office for a while. Love you. PS: Carole left new coffee for us to try.

After eating, she sat down to watch some mindless TV, but again fatigue overtook her. She retrieved a quilt and pillow from the closet and fell asleep on the couch, where she would find herself the next morning.

She showered, did a bit of laundry, and ate a light lunch, nodding off to sleep again while watching television. By late afternoon, she was feeling a bit more herself. Not great, but better. The UPS truck arrived, delivering two large boxes. Donna knew these were the records Russ Carotti had left behind. She sighed deeply. Not today. She wasn't ready for them today. She dragged them into her office, and closed the door, not even bothering to open them. There would be plenty of time for that tomorrow. Maybe.

She telephoned Carole. "It's about time we heard from you. I was just about to send out a rescue party, complete with a couple of Saint Bernard's with flasks around their necks," Carole boomed.

"They would have found me asleep, I assure you."

"Are you doing better? Is there anything you need?" her friend asked.

"Not a thing. I just wanted to thank you and Gavin for the treats you left in our fridge. They were a godsend."

"What are your plans, now that all this is behind you?"

"I need to go into the office tomorrow morning to meet with a client or two. For the time being, however, I'm going to spend most afternoons in my home office. I still have some questions that need answering. I'll fill you in when I can."

"Roger that. If you need a break, let me know. We'll do lunch."

At Donna's request, Ken brought a long table into her home office. She needed the extra desk space to organize the two boxes of records and journals. Her wall still contained the photos of the twenty-two victims. They would remain there until she finished her review.

Each numbered item was placed in order. It was obvious Russ Carotti, as exacting and precise as he was, wanted his story to unfold in a certain order so she would understand his motivation. So be it.

She began with a tattered book, a small journal, and spent the next hour reading every entry. The initial entry began the day after the Johnstown Flood, June 1, 1889. Donna realized it was the diary of Ira Rosenfeld, Julia's husband, the great-grandfather of Russell Carotti. Ira Rosenfeld had not only lost his wife, but six of his eight children, with a son and a daughter surviving the devastation.

Ira Rosenfeld's accountings were explicit, revealing a man barely holding onto his sanity. Vacillating between shock and rage, and the need for revenge, he, along with several others, stormed the South Fork Fishing and Hunting Club the day following the flood, intent on violently confronting the club members. With the place deserted, they imposed a trail of ruin upon the property as best they could. It was Ira who discovered a small box of gold pins engraved with a fishing toad in a desk drawer in the office of the caretaker, taking them without a word to anyone. They would be found years later by Ira Rosenfeld's great-grandson, Russell Carotti.

Donna, having finished her reading, put the diary to the side with a note to tell Jim it rightfully belonged to the museum, having been stolen years ago by Russell Carotti. Donna knew Carotti had visited the museum often, a fact proven by a request from Donna for copies of the guest rosters for the last twenty-five years. She surmised Carotti's plan of revenge was formulated as a result of his numerous visits to the museum. He never suspected his signing the guest roster each time could have been a conduit eventually for his identification as a killer. Then again, Russ Carotti was taunting the system to find him, and it failed until recently.

Donna moved on to other readings until she eventually came to Russ Carotti's diary. Like his great-grandfather before him, Russ's diary began with a specific date, December 31st, the day his wife and daughter were killed in a tragic car accident.

This was the validation Donna had been seeking, although she had been guessing up until now. Carotti had avenged his wife and child by avenging the flood victims. And while the date of his family's death was less than six months away from the yearly anniversary of the flood victims, he had achieved some sort of satisfaction in the anomaly.

The read was much the same as his great-grandfather's tragedy more than one hundred and twenty-five years earlier, the accounting of a man whose young wife and seven children had been torn from him so cruelly. Carotti, like his great-grandfather, was careful to include names, dates, and places in the aftermath of his loss.

Donna read on, shocked and deeply offended by the resulting insult levied against Carotti in the ensuing investigation into the death of his family. She understood the Croaker found no vindication from his loss. Instead, the unmitigated insult would unleash a squall of vengeance that would find its own form of justice for years to come.

"How are you coming along with things?" Ken asked several mornings later, when she entered the kitchen to the smell of coffee and bacon frying on the griddle. Donna was grateful for his patience these past several weeks. He was so very supportive.

"I'm almost there. I think I can write my report now."

Ken enfolded her in his arms and kissed her sweetly. "I am so very proud of you, Dear Heart. I know it's been rough."

Donna lay her head against his chest, taking in the scent of him, before speaking. "I keep going over the 'what ifs' in my mind, of which any one of them could have altered the turn of events." She looked up to kiss Ken endearingly.

"Ah! I sense the near return of my woman," he said jokingly.

"Soon. Very soon you will have the whole of me, and then some."

Donna spent the next several days in her office writing for Jim a detailed report of her investigative summary on the Croaker, not only from a professional viewpoint, but also from a personal one as well, a departure from her usual leaning.

Having completed the task, she emailed the report to Jim. Having done so, she felt a lightness she hadn't experienced in a very long time. It was time to return to the land of the living, she concluded, and with that thought she telephoned Carole.

"I'm letting you know I'm back in the saddle!" she announced to her best friend.

"It's about time! I was beginning to think you were sucked into the frog pond forever. We've missed you!"

"I've missed you! How about coming over tomorrow night for dinner? I feel festive again."

"We'll be there! I'll bring the coffee, and Gavin will bring dessert."

"We're a go!"

Chapter Twenty-Five

Donna pulled out all the stops for dinner with her mother's recipe for broccoli and cheese soup as an appetizer, followed by a beautifully prepared round rib roast with au jus, a delicate presentation of scalloped potatoes, and steamed, butter-seasoned asparagus spears.

Gavin and Carole were delighted to see the old Donna back again. The wine flowed freely before and through dinner. When everyone had pushed their plate away, they meandered into the living room to sit in front of the fireplace, enjoying after dinner drinks.

When the conversation experienced a lull, Donna cleared her voice. "I just want to thank you three for the support you've given me all this time. I couldn't have done it without you," she said, raising her glass in a toast.

"Here, here!" Carole boomed. "Is there anything about the Croaker case you found surprising?" Carole was just dying for the inside scoop.

It was just the introduction Donna needed. "Everything about this case was surprising, and even shocking. In the end, however, I came to understand Russ Carotti's motivation. Not that I agree with his method in any way. It's more of a heart-to-heart understanding, if you know what I mean."

"So he wasn't a sociopath?" Carole ventured.

Donna hesitated before she spoke. "I don't believe he was, based on a reading of his diary and journals. His mind took a turn that gave him permission to survive and endure. He wasn't an unfeeling monster. If anything, he had too much feeling, and took on too much responsibility to right the wrongs."

"What wrongs?" Gavin asked.

"I suspect Russ went into law enforcement with an idealistic bent. To get the bad guys. Then his wife and child were killed in a car accident. In the aftermath of his personal tragedy, the guilty party walked away, mainly because the person responsible for his family's death had connections. The guilty party was never held responsible for the crime."

"Who was the guilty party?" Ken asked, now on the edge of his seat.

Donna looked at Ken, Carole, and Gavin before responding. "Hold onto your hats. The drunk driver who plowed into Sarah Carotti, killing her and Russ's twelve-year-old daughter, Karen, New Year's Eve, all those years ago, was none other than George Heiser."

Ken stood immediately, almost spilling his drink. "What? No! You've got to be mistaken."

"I wish I were. I pulled the police reports from that day, along with all court actions thereafter. They confirm Heiser was the driver."

"How is it possible he was never held responsible?" Gavin asked, stunned by the revelation.

"The prosecutor was influenced by a newly-placed judge to drop the charges."

"No respecting judge would do such a thing. Unless they were on the take," Gavin added. "Who was the judge?"

"Judge Barrett Reeder."

"My God! No wonder Russ Carotti targeted this bastard, yet why wait twenty-two years?" Carole asked. "Why not take him out sooner?"

"I had to ask myself that same question. Russ's diary provided the answer, but not fully. My personal opinion is Russ never recovered from the demise of his family, and when the case against Heiser was dismissed, he found another way to survive, to make sense of the senseless. I believe this is when he took on the persona of an avenging angel for not only his loss, but also the loss of his family two generations before."

"He split off," Carole said, her previous career as a psychiatrist evident.

"Yes," Donna concurred.

"What does that mean?" Gavin asked, on the edge of his seat, his after-dinner drink forgotten.

"In terms of psychology, a splitting off indicates a departure from reality to take on the persona of another. In this case, Russ may have split off from his reality by taking on the persona of his raging great-grandfather of 1889. His unbridled grief at the loss of his family, along with the ensuing dismissal of the guilty party responsible for their deaths, propelled him into a rage so deep and so all encompassing, it created a kind of fissure in his mind, a leap into another period. It is at this point I believe, he became the guardian of the damned to those victims of the Johnstown Flood of 1889. It was then he believed he had to right the wrong, and bring justice to a situation where, until now, there had been no evidence of justice or blame. In doing so, he entered into the ever-present muddy puddle of the maelstroms of the silent…his deceased family.

"Another leaning in the Croaker's mind may have been the club members of 1889 were never held legally responsible for the loss of lives in the flood. The substantial wealth of the group as a whole would have made it difficult to get a settlement, although several residents tried.

"Add Mr. George Heiser to the scenario, another wealthy person who escaped indictment and prosecution because he could afford to. So Carotti, in order to deal with the unfathomable displacement of justice, targeted the still well-off descendants of previous club members."

The group remained quiet, digesting her summary. They were clearly unnerved.

"Just when did it all become clear?" Carole ventured forth. "At what point did you determine Russ Carotti was the Croaker?"

"There was a point when you came to my home to review the carpet samples for the cafés. Remember? We went into my office to get my glasses and you commented on the wall of victims and their dates of death. I remember asking myself why Carotti provided the dates of discovery of the bodies rather than the dates of death. That seemed odd to me. It was a fleeting thought, leaving my mind as quickly as it entered. I now see it as Carotti deliberately challenging investigators. Then on Christmas Eve, little Mary commented on Gavin's aftershave. It was then all the lights went on.

"You've got to be kidding?" Carole returned.

"You gave Gavin an aftershave for his birthday that would often give me a headache. My sensitivity to some scents remains a challenge. It was Mary's comment that started the ball rolling in my mind. It brought me to those recent occasions when I felt ill when subjected to a scent that disagreed with me. Bingo! The first time was in the Closet at the Pittsburgh investigative unit. I remember asking for the door to be opened because I was getting a headache. I was certain it was because the room was musky. Then the same response happened at the Johnstown Museum fundraiser shortly after the auction when Ken and I walked about to get a better look at the auctioned art pieces. I remember asking Ken to take me to the next tent to clear my head.

"Russ Carotti was in the Closet. He was also in the auction tent, though in disguise, wearing the same cologne and certainly near enough to create an allergic response. We now know Russ was not only a waiter at the fundraiser, but also a vehicle attendant as well. He admits as much in his diary. What he didn't know was his cologne would eventually be the catalyst for discovery.

"Then I began thinking of the circumstances that brought me into this investigation and realized all of Jim's information came from Russ Carotti and from Russ Carotti only. Jim and I had no reason to suspect anything was amiss. Carotti, before his retirement, transferred all his files over to Jim, plain and simple. Once I made the connection with the aftershave, however, I questioned whether Russ had controlled this situation right from the start. Believe me when I tell you, I was hoping I was dead wrong. That's when I had a long talk with Jim."

"He believed you?" Gavin asked.

"Not at first. In fact, he was more than a little peeved with me. He said, in no uncertain terms, I was going in the wrong direction and if he committed his team to any effort, he had to be certain. He was very clear he not only could not, but would not, be embarrassed given his short time on the Pittsburgh force. Eventually he came around, but it took me all night to convince him to at least think about my findings."

"So what was the straw that broke the camel's back for Jim?" Ken inquired.

"It was my questioning about the killing of Judge Reeder. Jim had earlier questioned why the Croaker had accelerated his timetable by more than six months, killing in June instead of December. Carotti provided the answer in his journals. He had surgery five months earlier. Stage four pancreatic cancer. It was too little, too late. The doctors gave him six months to live."

"So the judge had to go before he did," Carole concluded.

"That's about right. The catalyst for doing so, however, was far different from the previous twenty-one killings," Donna added.

"Why is that?" Gavin asked.

"Judge Barrett Reeder was the great-grandson of Edward Jay Allen, a South Fork Club member who was instrumental in the formation of the Pacific and Atlantic Telegraph Company. Carotti, however, did not know Reeder was the offspring of a club member until he started doing research on Edward Jay Allen in preparation for Victim Twenty-Three."

"Bingo!" Carole boomed, directing her comment to Donna.

"Exactly. This gave Carotti all the impetus he needed to right not one wrong, but two wrongs!"

"Now Carotti could avenge the Johnstown Flood victims of 1889 as well as the deaths of his wife and daughter," Ken said, shaking his head in disbelief and understanding.

No one spoke for a time, each evaluating the situation as well as the ongoing consequences.

"So he has less than six months to live, and discovers the man responsible for excusing George Heiser of vehicular manslaughter in the death of his young family twenty-six years earlier was a descendant of one of the sixty-one members of the South Fork Club. This is mind-blowing!" Carole almost yelled.

"The perfect storm," Donna replied quietly.

"More like a tsunami!" Carole added with her usual exuberance.

"Here's what I've been meaning to ask since Carotti's suicide that night," Ken interjected. "You had an exchange with Carotti at the cemetery the night of his death regarding Andrew Carnegie. It appeared to be significant. You seemed to understand his motivation, at least to a point."

Donna pondered Ken's position. "I am still in the throes of wrapping my mind around Carotti's psyche. His journals reveal his abhorrence toward the members of the South Fork Fishing and Hunting Club. They had wealth, power, and control. The club represented the sum total of absolute autonomy in its day by sheer force of member wealth. Remember, flood claims against the club were either dismissed, or died in the graveyard of legal proceedings, with the less-than-wealthy litigants unable to sustain the barrage of expense.

"Carnegie, however, was a departure for his time. Carotti understood this, even coming to respect the tycoon to some degree, judging by what he reveals in his journals. Carnegie was of a different bent, resolute in his belief that wealth was to be given away to causes. It is a fact, when he retired he devoted his remaining years to many efforts, in the hope that upon his death, there would be little left of his estate, except for those sums granted to his only daughter, Margaret Carnegie Miller."

"Wow! That's the kind of thing I like to hear," Carole replied enthusiastically.

"So that leaves George Heiser..." Gavin ventured further. "Why did Carotti not go after George Heiser? He certainly had every reason. After all, the guy was responsible for his family's death."

"Ah, yes! George Heiser," Donna countered for the benefit of her audience still in rapt attention. "I find George Heiser is a man of many faces. Cordial, gentlemanly, gracious, generous, stately, connected, and very wealthy, so it would seem, and a victim himself. The Croaker wanted Heiser to suffer."

"Suffer? In what way? George Heiser seems to have it all, money, position, and connections. It doesn't appear to me he is suffering," Gavin argued.

"Oh, but he is! And Russell Carotti knew this."

"Let me guess," Ken projected. "Reeder was holding George Heiser hostage for the favor of a dismissal of charges in the deaths of Carotti's family years before."

"Exactly! According to the journals, Heiser had been paying Reeder for years in the form of 'support funds' for one political candidate or another. Reeder was a big shot in politics. Anyone who wanted favor courted Reeder. Reeder, in turn, 'suggested' to Heiser payments to the candidate of Reeder's choice. Reeder controlled not only the elected candidates, but Heiser as well."

Donna continued. "Knowing Heiser was paying Reeder heavily via various political funding efforts, in Carotti's fiendish plotting processes, he found pleasure watching Heiser twist in the wind at the hands of Reeder. Heiser paid and paid dearly, until he couldn't pay anymore."

"The fundraiser was a high level event. It's inconceivable it was window dressing," Gavin countered in disbelief.

"Yes," Donna replied wearily. "The real facts have been hidden for some time now. It turns out George Heiser was decimated by the 2008 Great Recession. At the time, he was heavily invested in construction projects and firms related to the housing industry. When the construction and housing markets imploded as a consequence of the mortgage-backed security scheme, Heiser went down with the ship. For these last eight years, he's been living a lie, selling his artwork to raise money to keep afloat. Fortunately for him, the Heiser Bed and Breakfast does well, but he is petrified his insurmountable debt will be leaked."

"I'm guessing again," Ken interjected. "The drunken banker at the fundraiser, Keith Demoine, knew of Heiser's money issues."

"Yes, and Demoine was getting a bit too mouthy that evening about the lavish affair. Heiser had him ushered away as quickly as possible."

"God! What a cesspool!" Carole quipped.

"The crap, no pun intended, continues," Donna went on. "Heiser was forced to place much of his artwork as collateral to continue his lifestyle. His ruse couldn't have lasted, and the shit eventually hit the fan. Reeder wasn't getting his payoffs. It was causing a disconcerting drop in Reeder's sway in affairs of state. Heiser's investments were in the toilet. The whole carefully-contrived scheme was about to implode. For the Croaker, watching it all as an observer was better than a kill."

"So Reeder's bid on the artwork was a front," Ken assessed quickly.

"Yes. Reeder would look good for his generous donation toward the Johnstown Museum, but he would keep the artwork and sell it on the black market, thus Heiser would stave off uglier consequences, at least for a time. For Heiser, Reeder's death was a godsend, but he also knew an investigation would reveal the shady goings-on between the two, exposing Heiser on another level."

"The artwork was stolen, wasn't it?" Gavin asked.

"Yes, its whereabouts are unknown," Donna confirmed. "We assume Russ Carotti is responsible for its disappearance, but there is no mention of it in his journals."

"This would explain why Heiser was so upset regarding the loan history and his threat to sue for breach of privacy," Ken offered.

"Yes. He was more exposed than ever before," Donna concurred. "Now, it gets even more interesting."

"You've got *me* hooked!" Carole said, sitting literally on the edge of her seat.

"Thea Germaine is Judge Reeder's first wife."

"What?" Donna's audience of three said all at once.

"According to the journals, Thea and Russ dated in high school. He had a real thing for her. While he was away at college, however, she broke it off with him and married Barrett Reeder the following year. The marriage lasted less than three years, leaving Thea without a home or means of support. She took back her maiden name after the divorce and eventually went to school to secure a degree in business administration. It was George Heiser who suggested Thea for the position of administrator of the Johnstown Museum.

"By this point, Russ was married. Heiser and Germaine became an item, but never married. Though coming to hate Heiser for the death of his family, Carotti also viewed Heiser as the caretaker of Thea Germaine. Apparently, he retained high regard for Ms. Germaine."

"It seems to me the Croaker had an unusual understanding of dynamics and possible outcomes," Gavin reflected. "This was no shallow man."

"Indeed he did." Donna glanced at Ken before continuing. "The Croaker left two items in my care in the event of his death."

Gavin and Carole looked at each other. "They would be?" Gavin asked for the both of them.

"There was one large envelope with two life insurance policies in them, each in the amount of two hundred-fifty thousand dollars."

"Whew! Who are the lucky beneficiaries?" Carole asked.

"For one policy, the Johnstown Flood Museum is the beneficiary. Even in his death, he determined to be guardian of the damned," Donna replied.

"The other policy?" Gavin queried.

"There are two beneficiaries on this policy, each to get one half of the policy amount of another two hundred-fifty thousand dollars. One is Grandview Cemetery. His only request of Grandview is for them to provide a vault to hold the ashes of himself, his wife, and their child so they could all be together again, as well as flowers placed on the grave of Julia Rosenfeld and The Monument of Tranquility every May 31st."

"The anniversary of the Johnstown Flood," Carole affirmed.

Donna nodded her head. They all were quiet for a time, absorbing the unexpected turn of events.

"The second beneficiary?" Gavin finally probed.

"Bob Boykin," Donna replied quietly.

"Yoda?" Carole asked, more than a little surprised by the answer. "Why him?"

"Again, Mr. Carotti managed to be very precise in relaying his reasoning. It seems Boykin and Carotti are cousins."

"They look nothing alike," Ken observed.

"Apparently, they had been very close as children. When Carotti lost his family, Boykin was the guy Russ credited with pulling him through his darkest hours. Carotti, aware Heiser was in debt up to his eyeballs and behind in payments to Boykin for work done at the bed and breakfast, named Boykin as beneficiary knowing he would never be paid by Heiser."

"Do the beneficiaries know of these policies?" Gavin inquired.

"No. The Croaker asked Donna to deliver the policies to the beneficiaries," Ken answered testily. Ken was clearly not pleased by Donna's assignment.

"That's spooky!" Carole boomed. "The hairs on the back of my head stand up thinking of a serial killer using you to tie up his loose ends."

"Since it was a suicide, will the insurance company pay up? Gavin asked.

"I recently spoke with the insurance company and asked the same question. They called me back several days later to say that the policy would be honored."

"What's the other item?" Gavin asked.

"What?"

"You mentioned you were left with two items. The first item is the large envelope with the two insurance policies. What's the other item?"

Donna grew still. "The ashes of his wife and child."

Chapter Twenty-Six

Less than a week later, Donna received a phone call from Trudy Zimmerman, administrator of the Grandview Cemetery.

"Dr. DeShayne, I hope I'm not interrupting anything."

"No, of course not. It's good to hear from you. How can I be of assistance?"

"Detective Callahan contacted me this morning informing me that Grandview has been named as partial beneficiary in the estate of Mr. Russell Carotti. I understand you are holding the insurance policy."

"I am, Mrs. Zimmerman. I asked Jim to contact you first before I forward a copy."

The administrator hesitated before continuing. "I must admit, doctor; I was shocked by Mr. Carotti's suicide here on our grounds. More than that, I am shocked by the newspapers labeling Russ as a serial killer. Is there anything you can tell me? You seem to be involved in this matter."

"I understand your confusion and concern, but I am not at liberty to discuss the circumstances of Mr. Carotti's death or how I came to have possession of the insurance policy. Detective Callahan can answer all of your questions and will be releasing more details, I can assure you. How well did you know Russell Carotti, if I may ask?"

"We've known each other for years. We went to school together. It's a small town. Russ just isn't capable of the kind of violence he's accused of. Can you at least tell me who the second named beneficiary is on the policy?"

"That would be Bob Boykin."

"I see. Bob and Russ were very close."

"Mrs. Zimmerman—"

"Please, there is no need for formality. Call me Trudy."

"Perhaps you can help me. I'm aware he lost his family tragically in a car accident some years back. Did you see a change in him after the event, Trudy?"

"Oh, yes. He was not the same man I grew up with after the loss of his family. He nearly went mad with grief. Bob was scared Russ would take his own life. He never left his side. Eventually, Russ seemed to stabilize, but remained distant and reserved. There was an edge to him. He stopped attending the yearly reunions and other get-togethers. It was as if he was avoiding his former life. I eventually lost track of him. I would send Christmas cards every year, but he never acknowledged them. Then I get a phone call informing me of his suicide on cemetery grounds."

"Would you know what Mr. Carotti's major was in college?"

"It is a curious question, doctor, but I will answer. He majored as a chemical engineer, but dropped out after a year to go into law enforcement. Is that important?"

"Somewhat. What kind of relationship did Mr. Carotti and Mr. Heiser have growing up?"

"Not much of one. Heiser's family had money. Most of us, including Russ, came from the other side of the tracks."

"I see."

"Why do you ask?"

"Mr. Heiser appears to have a prominent place in the affairs of the area. I thought maybe Mr. Carotti and he would have had more interaction with each other, is all. They both had an interest in the same woman."

"Thea Germaine. Yes. I wouldn't call that a reason for continuing interaction between the two men, however. Thea's relationship with Russ ended decades ago. I take it you are seeking more information than you are willing to share yourself."

Donna wasn't expecting the administrator to be so direct. "It would be inappropriate for me to do so. I can assure you, however, I will be sending a copy of the insurance policy. Can you provide the address of Bob Boykin?"

The doctor and the administrator exchanged parting pleasantries before ending the call. Donna was already planning her next visit to Johnstown.

Several weeks before her planned visit to Johnstown, Donna received a phone call from Jim. "I just got word from the Johnstown police and thought you would like to know," Jim said.

"What is it?"

"George Heiser died of a stroke sometime during the night. He was found by Thea Germaine this morning. She became concerned when he didn't answer her calls or texts and decided to stop by the bed and breakfast to check on him. Fortunately, there were no guests."

"Oh, do you suspect any foul play?"

"Not at this point. Ms. Germaine indicated Heiser was under doctor's care recently for a heart issue. There was talk of a pacemaker as part of his treatment. They'll be talking with his doctor this afternoon."

"This may sound silly, but after all the issues with the Croaker case, and knowing what we know now, I would be suspicious of Heiser's death if it wasn't for the fact Russ Carotti is dead."

"I went through the same mental gymnastics, I assure you. I'm certain Heiser's death is a coincidence. We'll be seeing you and Ken in a couple of weeks," Jim said, changing the subject. "Karly and I are looking forward to your visit."

"We're looking forward to getting the loose ends behind us. Thanks for allowing us to stay at your place again."

"After we get business out of the way, we can put this all behind us and spend some time in the city again."

"We'd love that!"

Ken and Donna arrived in Pittsburgh two days before the anniversary of the flood on an early morning flight. Jim and Karly met them at the airport, taking them to a favorite breakfast restaurant they'd discovered since Ken and Donna's last visit. They then headed for Johnstown to spend the next two nights; at the same motel they used on their previous visit.

For both Donna and Jim, there was unfinished business in the Croaker affair. They were hoping to resolve one of those issues today.

"Everything's set. All we have to do is watch and wait," Jim announced to Donna.

She nodded. The next morning she and Jim arrived very early at the Johnstown Flood Museum three hours before it opened. They placed themselves behind a wall where a peephole had been discreetly installed the day before. It would allow them a good view of the hallway.

Finally, Thea Germaine entered the building at the usual time, looked about and went straight to her office, unlocking the door. Looking down at her feet, she was disappointed, but relieved at the same time. Jim and Donna came up behind her. She turned toward them before speaking, still scanning the floor.

"Nothing," was all she said.

"We had to try," Jim returned.

"So are we to assume there is to be no altered list of the dead this year because Russ Carotti is dead?" the curator asked.

"If it was Carotti who slipped the list under your door each year, then, yes, I think we can assume this yearly overture has ended."

"I'm still puzzled," Donna interjected. "If it was Carotti, he had to have had a key to the building to let himself in."

"Not necessarily," Jim countered. "Don't forget, Carotti was in law enforcement. He probably picked the lock, let himself in, slipped the list under the door, and made his way out again, locking the door behind him. It would take less than a minute."

"You'll let us know if this list presents itself again?" Jim told, rather than asked, the curator.

"Yes, by all means," Thea assured him.

Donna observed how haggard Thea looked. She surmised the death of George Heiser was still heavy on her heart. Placing her hand on the woman's arm, Donna offered her sympathy. "We're so sorry for your loss, Ms. Germaine. We appreciate how much support Mr. Heiser was to the museum. I'm sure this town will miss him."

The curator teared up, unable to speak. Donna embraced the woman for a time before releasing her to her office where she simply closed the door quietly behind her without another word.

They would find out months later that the Heiser Bed and Breakfast was sold at auction to raise money to cover Heiser's insurmountable debt. Most of the artwork was auctioned off as well, bringing a fraction of what it was worth. The news had gotten out that most of it was collateralized. George Heiser died broken and broke.

Chapter Twenty-Seven

Donna, Ken, Jim, and Karly arrived early at the cemetery the next day and immediately went to the office to announce their arrival. Within minutes Trudy Zimmerman came from a back room to greet them. Introductions were made before getting down to the business at hand.

"I want to say something before we begin," Trudy announced with a slight tremor.

"By all means," Donna returned softly. She noticed Trudy's hands were shaking; her face pale.

"As I have already conveyed a while back, I was deeply disturbed to learn of the circumstances surrounding the death of Russ Carotti. This is not the Russ Carotti I knew. I visited his home often. I got to know his family and simply loved his mother, Ruth. She, unfortunately, married a bastard after Russ's father died. I would often see the bruises on her face, and that of her son."

Trudy lowered her head. It was obviously difficult for her to continue. "I beg you not to judge Russ harshly. His mind became twisted after the death of his family, but I assure you his heart was, at its core, a good one. His grief can be the only explanation for the unspeakable acts he has been accused of." The administrator raised her head and looked Jim straight in the eyes. "Are you absolutely sure Russ Carotti is this person you are calling the Croaker?"

Donna looked at Jim. He understood and nodded. She then stepped forward toward the lifelong friend of the Croaker. "I regret how painful this must be for you," Donna ventured forth, carefully choosing her words, her voice remaining subdued. "However, by his own written hand, he admitted to the killing of twenty-two people, each one a descendant of a member of the South Fork Fishing and Hunting Club. I believe, upon the death of his family, he had to transcend his grief and create another enemy, or go completely mad. He chose an alternate existence. He saw himself as the avenger of the two thousand two hundred nine flood victims whose deaths were never acknowledged with retribution. The death of his own family, never justifiably adjudicated, fanned the flames of insanity.

"I agree he may have been a good person at one point. In our society, however, murder is wrong. The murder of twenty-two innocent people is very wrong, regardless of the background story. We cannot herald an injustice. We can only try to understand the pain and rage that preceded it."

Trudy Zimmerman seemed to wilt and draw into herself. She stood motionless, unsettled by the reality check Donna conveyed.

It took a moment or two, but Trudy, much to her credit, gathered herself into a professional stance and setting. "I will go back to my office to retrieve Russ's remains. I will meet you here and then we can walk together the rest of the way. I took the liberty of asking my minister to say a prayer. He should be here shortly. By the way, until this week I had no idea Russ had picked out a drawer and its location years ago. Those matters are left for another department in our firm."

"How did you find out?"

"Bob Boykin. Apparently Russ told him of the arrangement years before. When I looked it up on the computer, sure enough, there it was." Trudy turned and walked away.

Donna suddenly felt tired and turned toward Ken for support. The dynamics of the occasion had come down to this very hour where she would join Russ's ashes with those of his deceased family.

Ken drew his arms around her protectively. "You have just a little bit more to go, sweetie, and then your job is done."

They both walked back to the car to retrieve the urns of Sarah and Karen Carotti. Jim and Karly remained where they were. On their walk back to the office, they noted the minister had arrived. Trudy returned with the ashes of Russell Carotti, led the group to the far end of the cemetery, and then stopped.

"It looks like Bob was here," she said.

"How do you know?" Donna asked.

"The flowers are already in the holder. It wasn't us who put them there, so it must have been Bob. He arranged for an identification plate as well." The plaque listed the names of the deceased, Russell Carotti, Sarah Carotti, and Karen Carotti, along with dates of birth and death.

Trudy opened the drawer and nodded to the minister. He cleared his throat before saying a few words and ending with a prayer. From the corner of her eye, Donna caught movement behind her. Turning slightly so as not to draw attention, she saw Bob Boykin standing solemnly a distance away, with tears streaming down his face. When she looked back again, he was gone.

When the minister finished, Trudy placed the ashes of Russ into the drawer and nodded for Donna to do the same. Once the ashes of Sarah and Karen Carotti were placed beside those of Russell Carotti, the door was closed and sealed.

"I promised to show you the plot of Julia Rosenfeld the next time you visited. Would you still like to see it?" Trudy asked.

"I would," Donna replied.

The administrator turned around and walked a step or two forward. "Julia Rosenfeld," was all she said, directing her gaze to a plot with flowers. "As you can see, we are adhering to Russ's request for flowers to be placed on his great-grandmother's gravesite every May 31st. You will find flowers at the Monument of Tranquility as well."

"Oh, dear!" Donna exclaimed. "She is directly across from Russ and his family's vault!"

"Interesting, isn't it? The records indicate Russ purchased this particular site shortly after the death of his family. It's been waiting all this time for the four of them to be together again."

The group said their goodbyes to Trudy and made their way back to their vehicle, but not before stopping at the Monument of Tranquility to see the flowers arranged and placed by the cemetery.

Once in the car, Donna let out a huge sigh. "It's done," was all she said, immensely relieved the Croaker case had been settled once and for all. She snuggled up beside Ken, grateful for his support and love. He kissed her softly.

"You did an outstanding job, Donna," Jim said over his shoulder, now behind the wheel of the vehicle. "I couldn't have done this without you, that's for sure."

"Are all the loose ends tied up, then?" Karly asked as they drove out of the parking lot.

"All, except the whereabouts of the artwork Reeder bid on at the auction. We may never know what happened to it," was Jim's reply. "At this point, it doesn't really matter. Someday it will resurface, but probably not on my watch."

Bob Boykin returned to his apartment, feeling lonelier than ever before. The loss of his cousin hit him hard, especially when he learned Russ was a killer they were calling the Croaker. Russ was the only family he'd had left. It was Russ who had protected him against the bullies all his life. Now he was gone.

He made a strong cup of coffee before settling into an aging upholstered chair in the living room. He picked up the note on the side table that was attached to the package left at the back door earlier in the year.

Bob,

Do a favor and hold onto this for me. If I don't come back for it after a time, consider it yours. In the meantime, put it someplace where you can enjoy it.

It will fetch a good price. Russ

Bob Boykin looked at the wall in front of him. He smiled and understood. Russ was watching out for him even in death. The stolen Leonid Afremov artwork took a prominent place in Bob's home. For years to come it would rest on the wall, with no one the wiser. A gift from the Croaker.

"...The LORD, the LORD God, merciful and gracious, long-suffering, and abundant in goodness and truth.

Keeping mercy for thousands, forgiving iniquity and transgression and sin, and that will by no means clear the guilty; visiting the iniquity of the fathers upon the children, and upon the children's children, unto the third and to the fourth generation."

—Exodus 34: 6, 7 - The Gideon Bible

A Bella Fayre Overview

A great many fictional liberties were taken in the writing of *Guardian of the Damned*. In no way should the reader regard the history of the Johnstown Flood of 1889, when used as background in a fictional setting, as an attempt to discredit, disrespect, or disregard the deceased or their offspring. A diligent attempt was made to include factual information to refresh the reader's mind about the tragic events that transpired more than one hundred twenty-five years ago. These would include, but not be limited, to the following:

- The official number of dead from the flood remains at two thousand two hundred nine.
- The South Fork Fishing and Hunting Club was an exclusive club for the wealthy, purchased and organized as a retreat for their members ten years before the flood. The sixteen charter members were: Henry Clay Frick, Benjamin Ruff, T.H. Sweat, Charles J. Clarke, Thomas Clark, Walter F. Fundenberg, Howard Hartley, Henry C. Yeager, J.B. White, E.A. Myers, C.C. Hussey, D.R. Ewer, C.A. Carpenter, W.L. Dunn, W.L. McClintock, and A.V. Holmes. Eventual membership total would be sixty-one.
- Andrew Carnegie, a member of the club, was a generous benefactor in relief efforts, contributing a new library for Johnstown. Carnegie never visited the club. His name does not appear on any guest register in the club's ten-

year history. His brother Thomas visited on more than one occasion.

- Daniel Johnson Morrell, general manager of Cambria Iron Company and Club member, warned of questionable conditions related to the dam by providing his own engineering report. The report and its warnings went unheeded.
- Cambria Iron Works was established in 1848, nearly fifty years before the flood, and became one of the nation's largest producer of rails. Immigrants from Southern and Eastern Europe came to Johnstown to work at the steel plant. In 1989, the Cambria Iron Works Complex was designated a National Historic Landmark. The plant eventually closed in 1992.
- It took less than one hour from the time the dam broke at 2:55 PM on May 31st for twenty million tons of waters to rush at a speed comparable to that of Niagara Falls, to reach Johnstown, Pennsylvania.
- Ninety-nine entire families perished, three hundred ninety-six children under the age of ten died, and five hundred sixty-eight children lost one or both parents. It is estimated the flood left one hundred ninety-eight husbands without wives and one hundred twenty-four wives without husbands.
- Members of the South Fork Fishing and Hunting Club were never held legally responsible for the catastrophe. Several attempts at lawsuits were either abandoned or dismissed.

- The club did have an official seal depicting a fishing toad. It can be viewed at the Johnstown Flood Museum.
- Victor Heiser, losing both parents in the deluge, left Johnstown at the age of sixteen one year later. He went on to attend medical school, devoting his life to fighting disease around the world. He would later be credited with his contribution toward a cure for leprosy. Victor Heiser is buried at Grandview Cemetery. George Heiser was the name of Victor Heiser's father. However, George Heiser in the novel is purely a fictional character. To my knowledge, there is no Heiser House Bed and Breakfast in the Johnstown area.
- The Johnstown Flood Museum and the Johnstown Area Heritage Association provide a wealth of information on this event.
- The National Park Service oversees the Johnstown Flood National Memorial in South Fork, Pennsylvania, including the South Fork Fishing and Hunting Club as well as three of the nine remaining cottages. The park service offers *Path of the Flood* van tours and hikes of approximately four hours in duration. It is well worth the visit. The clubhouse is slated for restoration.
- The Grandview Cemetery remains a remarkable tribute to the memory of those who perished in the Great Johnstown Flood. Its impressive Monument of Tranquility along with the Unknown Plot are sober reminders of the toll this disaster took on those impacted by the tragedy.

Suggested Readings

For a thorough historical perspective, the following writings are recommended by the Johnstown Area Heritage Association:

1. *The Johnstown Flood*, by David McCullough - Copyright 1968
2. *The 1889 Flood in Johnstown, Pennsylvania* by Dr. Michael R. McGough - Copyright 2002
3. *Through the Johnstown Flood by a Survivor* by Dr. Rev. David J. Beale
4. *The Story of Johnstown* by J. J. McLaurin

Acknowledgments

In the author's opinion, no one accomplishes anything of significance without the support of others. To that end, I wish to express my appreciation and gratitude to the following for their willing support and contribution toward the completion of *Guardian of the Damned*. I bow to their expertise:

- Ms. Kaytlin Sumner, Curator of the Johnstown Heritage Association, Johnstown, Pennsylvania, for her generous and gracious overview during my visit to the Johnstown Flood Museum and in answering my questions related to flood history in the course of my writing.
- Mr. Mark J. Duray, President and COO, Citizens Cemetery Association (Grandview Cemetery), for permission to make use of current artwork for the cover of *Guardian of the Damned.*
- Mr. Nathan Koozer—National Park Service Ranger whose summary and knowledge on the *Path of the Flood* van tour as provided by the Johnstown Flood National Memorial, South Fork, Pennsylvania, proved invaluable. It was a fact-filled adventure.
- The Carolina Forest Author's Club of Myrtle Beach, South Carolina, for their gracious editing suggestions and encouragement toward final completion. They are a wonderfully talented and delightful group. I am honored to count them among my friends.

- Ms. Elizabeth "Shay" VanZwoll, EV Proofreading, for review and related suggestions.
- Ms. Jessica Tilles, TWA Solutions, for professional services related to editing, interior placement, and book cover design.
- Mr. Matt Carson, for his overview of insurance policies as related to suicide.
- Detective Ron Meinecke, for his review on jurisdictional precedence on murders committed over state lines as well as transfer of documents.
- Kathyrn Dunker for manuscript review and suggestions.

About the Author

Bella Fayre, a former resident of New Jersey, enjoys traveling, reading, and spending time with her granddaughter. She currently resides in South Carolina.

Other works by Bella Fayre

Maelstroms of the Silent

Made in the USA
Columbia, SC
17 March 2019